Dedalus European Classics
General Editor: Timothy Lane

THE CONTINUATION OF
SIMPLICISSIMUS

D1608066

*Johann Jakob Christoffel von
Grimmelshausen*

THE CONTINUATION OF SIMPLICISSIMUS

translated and with an introduction
by Mike Mitchell

Dedalus

Supported using public funding by
ARTS COUNCIL
ENGLAND

Published in the UK by Dedalus Limited
24-26, St Judith's Lane, Sawtry, Cambs, PE28 5XE
email: info@dedalusbooks.com
www.dedalusbooks.com

ISBN printed book 978 1 910213 92 6
ISBN ebook 978 1 912868 15 5

Dedalus is distributed in the USA & Canada by SCB Distributors
15608 South New Century Drive, Gardena, CA 90248
email: info@scbdistributors.com   web: www.scbdistributors.com

Dedalus is distributed in Australia by Peribo Pty Ltd
58, Beaumont Road, Mount Kuring-gai, N.S.W. 2080
email: info@peribo.com.au

Publishing History
First published in Germany in 1669
First published by Dedalus in 2019

The Continuation of Simplicissimus translation and introduction copyright
© *Mike Mitchell 2019*

The right of Mike Mitchell to be identified as the editor & translator of this
work has been asserted by him in accordance with the Copyright, Designs
and Patents Act, 1988.

Printed and bound in Great Britain by Clays Ltd, Elcograf S.p.A
Typeset by Marie Lane

A C.I.P. listing for this book is available on request.

The Translator

For many years an academic with a special interest in Austrian literature and culture, Mike Mitchell has been a freelance literary translator since 1995.

He has published over eighty translations from German and French, including Gustav Meyrink's five novels and *The Dedalus Book of Austrian Fantasy*. His translation of Rosendorfer's *Letters Back to Ancient China* won the 1998 *Schlegel-Tieck Translation Prize* after he had been shortlisted in previous years for his translations of *Stephanie* by Herbert Rosendorfer and *The Golem* by Gustav Meyrink.

His translations have been shortlisted four times for *The Oxford Weidenfeld Translation Prize*: *Simplicissimus* by Johann Grimmelshausen in 1999, *The Other Side* by Alfred Kubin in 2000, *The Bells of Bruges* by Georges Rodenbach in 2008 and *The Lairds of Cromarty* by Jean-Pierre Ohl in 2013.

What is the life of man? Inconstancy its name,
When we think we're settled, we must go on again.
O most fickle state! Thinking we're at rest
All at once the Fall – comes us to molest,
Just as Death comes. Read what such changeful ways
Have done to me in this chronicle of my days,
From which it can be seen that uncertainty
Alone is certain, wherever we may be.

Introduction

Grimmelshausen was born in 1622 – six years before John Bunyan, with whom there are interesting similarities and differences. Both came from impoverished backgrounds – Grimmelshausen put the noble *von* back in his name once he had become well-known as a writer – and managed to get some basic schooling before they were drawn into the wars of the time at an early age: Grimmelshausen at twelve, Bunyan at sixteen, and both confessed to 'all manner of vice and ungodliness' in their youth. Bunyan is best known for works in the allegorical mode and Grimmelshausen, while he is most remembered for his realism, also wrote two moralising works, which are mentioned in the 'Conclusion', and the *The Continuation* of *Simplicissimus* is full of Christian piety, though Grimmelshausen is writing from a Catholic viewpoint, having gone over to the Imperial side during the wars.

In fact, the *Continuation* could be called Grimmelshausen's 'pilgrim's progress'. At the end of *Simplicissimus* the hero withdraws from the world and goes to live as a hermit in the Black Forest. As in Bunyan's allegory, Grimmelshausen's *Continuation* also starts with a dream, though a dream of the hero not the author, which is allegorical: he dreams of Hell with the devil and all his minions, who are the personifications of the vices that lead men to Hell. After he wakes he resolves to abandon his solitary life and become a holy pilgrim and makes his way, with various adventures, to Italy, then to Egypt and, captured by Arab robbers, to the Red Sea. It is here that what is the most interesting part of the *Continuation* starts: having taken passage on a Portuguese merchant ship to return to Europe via Cape Horn, he is shipwrecked on a desert Island – almost sixty years before *Robinson Crusoe*. It is a fruitful island, a veritable paradise, and after the death of his companion, the ship's carpenter, he resolves to stay there in his life of solitary piety, even when a Dutch ship, that has been driven off course, offers him a chance of returning home.

Simplicissimus, published in 1668, though dated 1669, was a great success and Grimmelshausen immediately followed it with a number of other books that are generally referred to as his 'Simplician Writings': *The Continuation* was added to the original as the 'Sixth Book'; *Courage, Tearaway* and four other short works were published over the next few years.

The desert-island episode is presented as a report from the captain of the Dutch ship to the writer German Schleiffheim von Sulsfort of his meeting with the hermit, in which he also claims Simplicissimus gave him an account of his whole life, written by the hermit on palm leaves with ink made from lemon juice and the sap of fernambuco wood. The final 'Conclusion' after this is a note from H. I. C. V. G. (ie Hans Jacob Christoffel von Grimmelshausen) asserting that the book was found among the papers of Samuel Greifsnon vom Hirschfeld after his death and that he was the author of *Simplicissimus* but had used an anagram of his name on the title page: German Schleifheim von Sulsfort.

This is one final mystification from Grimmelshausen. He published his 'Simplician writings' under the pseudonym of 'German Schleifheim von Sulsfort' (Cornelissen's misspelling of Schleiffheim is probably a misprint, or a further mystification). 'Samuel Greifsnon vom Hirschfeld' who is here presented as the 'real author' is not quite an anagram of 'German Schleifheim von Sulsfort' – there is a 'd' instead of a 't', though they tend to be regarded as interchangeable, since in German final 'd' is pronounced as 't'. However, if you look at the last three words of Grimmelshausen's name above, you will see that 'German Schleifheim von Sulsfort' is a perfect anagram.

Chapter 1

If anyone should imagine I am telling the story of my life in order to help people pass the time or, like clowns and buffoons, to make people laugh, then they are very much mistaken! Excessive laughter is something that disgusts me, and anyone who lets the precious, irrevocable hours slip by unused is wasting that divine gift that was given us to work for the salvation of our souls. Why should I encourage such vain foolishness and waste my time giving people entertaining advice to no purpose? As if I didn't know that in so doing I would be participating in other people's sins. I think myself somewhat too good for such a task, dear reader. So anyone who wants a fool for that should buy two, then he will always be able to make fun of one of them. I may occasionally put on a jester's cap but that is only for the sake of those tender souls who cannot swallow wholesome pills unless they be mixed with plenty of sugar and coated. Not to mention that even the most earnest of men, when they have to read serious writings will tend to put one book down rather than another that brings an occasional smile to their lips.

I may perhaps also be accused of taking a too satirical approach, but I cannot be blamed for that because most people prefer the common vices to be dealt with and castigated in general rather than have their own failings given friendly correction. Thus at the moment Mr Everyman, to whom this my story is addressed, is unfortunately not so fond of the theological pen that I should use it. That is the kind of thing you can see in a huckster or a quack (who call themselves renowned doctors or oculists, claim to be able to cure hernias or the stone and even have parchments with seals attesting that) when they appear in the open market with their merry-andrew or jack-pudding, whose first cry and fantastic capers attract a greater crowd of listeners than the most enthusiastic divine ringing all the bells three times to offer his flock a fruitful, salutary sermon.

However that may be, I hereby publicly declare that it is not my fault if someone should be annoyed because I have decked out my Simplicissimus in the way people demand if you want to teach them something useful. If, however, this or that reader should be content with the husk and ignore the core concealed with in it, they will be happy with an entertaining story. But although that will be far from fulfilling the real intention of this narrative, I am now starting again from where I left off at the end of the Fifth Book.

There the reader will have learnt that I had become a hermit once more and also why that happened; it is, therefore, now appropriate for me to relate what I then did. During the first few months, while it continued to be warm, things went very well. It took no great effort to suppress the urges of the flesh, to which I had been much addicted, for since I was no longer in thrall to Bacchus and Ceres, Venus too refused to come to me. But I was still far from perfect, a thousand temptations assailed me every hour and when I sought to recall my old wanton ways, in order to arouse a feeling of remorse, the pleasures of the flesh that I had enjoyed in this or that place immediately came to mind as well which was neither healthy nor served my spiritual progress. When I now recall the past and think things over, it is clear to me that idleness was my greatest enemy and freedom (because I had no priest to watch over and guide me) the reason why I did not continue in the life I had started out on.

I lived on a high mountain called the Mooskopf, in the Black Forest, covered all over in dark pinewoods. From there I had a beautiful view: to the east of the valley of Oppenau and its surroundings, to the south of the Kinzig valley and the county of Geroldseck where the high castle among the surrounding mountains looks like the king-pin in a set of skittles; to the west I could see Upper and Lower Alsace and to the north the low-lying margravate of Baden, down the River Rhine to where the city of Strasbourg, with its high cathedral tower, stands resplendent like a heart surrounded by its body. With such a view and sights to be seen I spent more time delighting in them than devoting myself to prayer, and my telescope, that I had not yet abandoned, certainly encouraged me in this. When I couldn't use it because of the nocturnal darkness, I took the instrument I had invented to improve my hearing and used it to listen to a farmer's dog barking several hours distance away or a wild animal moving close by. These were the foolish things with which I passed my time, gradually giving up work and prayer – the two things with which the old Egyptian hermits satisfied both their bodily and spiritual needs. At the beginning, when I was still new there, I went from house to house in the adjoining valleys seeking alms to support myself, not taking more than enough to supply my bare needs. In particular I spurned money, which greatly surprised the people in the vicinity; indeed, they even saw it as evidence of my sanctity. Once it became known where I lived, no forest-dweller would come into the woods without bringing me something to eat. They also praised my sanctity and unusual hermit's way of life in other places, so that people living somewhat farther away would, either out of curiosity or devoutness, make the effort to come and see me, bringing their offerings. Thus I had no lack but an abundance of bread, butter, salt, cheese, ham, eggs and the like. But that did not make me any more pious; the longer it went on the more dilatory and worse I became, so that I could almost have been called a hypocrite or a holy rogue. But I didn't give up thinking about virtue and vice, and wondering what I should do if I wanted to go to Heaven. But it was all disorganised, without honest advice and the firm resolution to pursue this with the seriousness my situation and its improvement demanded of me.

Chapter 2

We can read how, a long time ago, for the saintly members of the Christian church who were devoted to God the mortification of the flesh consisted mainly of praying, fasting and nightly vigils. However, I practised the first two very little and would also let myself straightway be overcome by the sweet torpor of sleep whenever I felt I was due to pay that debt to nature that we share with all animals. Once, when I was lazing in the shade of a pine tree, musing over idle thoughts as to whether greed or extravagance was the greatest or worst vice, I said: my idle thoughts! And I still say so today for, my dear friend, what concern was extravagance to me, who had nothing to be extravagant with? And what was greed to me since my very way of life, that I had chosen of my own free will, demanded that I should live in poverty and indigence? But oh, in my foolish way I was so determined to resolve that question that I couldn't put these thoughts out of my mind and fell asleep over them.

Now it is generally the case that the things we are occupied with while we are awake, come to plague our dreams, and that was what happened to me then. For hardly had I closed my eyes than I saw Lucifer, the grand duke of Hell, in a horrendously deep gorge. He was sitting on his ruler's throne, but bound with a chain, so that he couldn't impose his will on the world, but the obsequious attentions of the many fiendish spirits surrounding him were enough to attest to his infernal power.

While I was watching these courtiers, a swift messenger came flying through the air, knelt down before Lucifer and said, "O great Prince, the German peace that has been concluded has calmed almost the whole of Europe down. Everywhere the *Gloria in excelsis Deo* and the *Te Deum laudamus* ring out to the Heavens and all the people will now do their utmost to serve God under their vines or their fig trees."

As soon as Lucifer heard this news he was at first horrified, for he very much begrudged mankind this happiness. But once he had recovered himself a little and worked out what damage this would do to the advantages his hellish empire had so far enjoyed, he fell into a terrible ill-humour and ground his teeth so horribly that the fearsome sound was to be heard far and wide, his eyes blazed with such anger and impatience that they sent out fiery, sulphurous flames like bolts of lightning, filling his whole residence. Not only the poor humans who had been condemned to Hell and the minor demons were horrified by this but even his most noble princes and privy councillors. Finally he rammed the rocks with his horns, making the whole of Hell quiver, and started to rant and rave so furiously that his entourage could only imagine he would either stop completely or go quite out of his mind. The result was that for a while no one dared to approach him, even less to say a single word to him.

Eventually the demon Belial was bold enough to

say, "Mighty Prince, what is all this fuss for one of such incomparable majesty? What? Has the lord of lords forgotten himself? What are we to make of this unusual behaviour, that can be neither useful nor add to the renown of your glorious majesty?"

"O!" Lucifer replied, "O! O! We have all been asleep and through our own idleness allowed *Lerna malorum*, our favourite plant, that we made such an effort to establish on earth and the fruits of which we gathered with such great profit, has now been cleared out of the German lands and, unless we do something about it, will be eradicated from the whole of Europe. And yet not one of you all is taking that to heart. Is it not a disgrace that we are allowing the few days left to the world to pass in such slipshod fashion? You gawping sleepyheads, do you not realise that we should be reaping our richest harvest during these last days? That will make a fine mess of the end of the world if we are going to be like old dogs, moody and incapable of hunting; the beginning and continuation of the war brought us the bumper crop we hoped for straightaway, but what do we have to look forward to now that Mars, who usually has *Lerna malorum* following hard on his heels, has left Europe, apart from Poland?"

Once he had bellowed rather than said this, such was his malice and anger, he was about to fall into his former raving, but Belial held him back, saying, "We must not lose heart because of this, nor behave like weak men when they feel an unpleasant wind blowing. Don't you remember, great Prince, that more of them fall through wine than by the sword? Will not a quiet peace, bringing lust on its back, be more harmful to mankind, especially the Christians, than war? Is it not well known that the virtues of the Bride of Christ never shine more brightly than in the midst of the greatest tribulations?"

"It is, however," Lucifer replied, "my desire and my determination that men should spend their lives on earth in constant adversity and be in eternal torment after their death, but our negligence will eventually mean that they will enjoy well-being on earth and, what is more, eternal bliss afterwards."

"Huh!" Belial replied. "We both know how I work with little rest and will make such an effort to fulfil your determination and desire that *Lerna malorum* will stay even longer in Europe – or I'll give the lady something else to worry about. But Your Majesty must also remember that I can accomplish nothing if you grant the divine power to another."

Chapter 3

The friendly chat between the two infernal spirits was so vehement and furious that it set off an uproar throughout Hell with the result that the whole infernal host immediately gathered round in order to hear what was to be done: Lucifer's first child, Pride and her daughters, Greed with his brood, Wrath together with Envy and Hatred, Vindictiveness, Malevolence, Calumny and all their other relations, then Lust with his followers – Gluttony, Sloth and such – also Laziness, Perfidy, Wantonness, Duplicity, Forwardness that makes maidens attractive, Deceit and her charming little daughter Flattery, who was carrying a fox's tail in place of a fan. In fact it was a bizarre procession and strange to see since each came in their own strange garb: some magnificently attired, others in beggars' rags, and a third group, such as Shamelessness and the like, who were almost completely naked. Some were as fat and corpulent as Bacchus, others as yellow, pale and lean as a skinny old carthorse; yet others looked as lovely and charming as Venus while other groups were as surly as Saturn, as fierce as Mars, as sly and furtive as Mercury, as strong as Hercules, as erect and fast as Hippomenes or as limp and lame as Vulcan – all in all there was such a collection of different types and attire you could imagine it was the wild army the ancients told us so much about. And apart from the above-mentioned there were many more I could not recognise nor name, since some had come masked and disguised.

Lucifer gave a very sharp speech to this huge gathering in which he rebuked each one individually and the band as a whole for their negligence and told them in no uncertain terms that it was because of their slackness that the *Lerna malorum* had had to leave Europe. At the same time he made Sloth step forward and, calling him a useless bastard who was ruining his followers, banished him from his infernal kingdom forever and ordered him to go and take up his abode somewhere on earth.

After that he earnestly encouraged the rest to make greater efforts than they had so far to surreptitiously establish themselves among mankind, at the same time uttering terrible threats of the punishments he would visit on those who showed the least sign of not carrying out their duties with the fervour he demanded. He then handed out new instructions and memoranda, promising substantial rewards to those who proved to be hardworking.

When it looked as if this gathering was about to end and the whole hierarchy of Hell would go back to their business, a tattered and very pale-faced fellow rode in on an old, mangy wolf. Both the man and his steed looked so starved, haggard, weary and emaciated, as if the two of them had spent a long time lying in a grave or the knacker's yard. He was complaining about a stately lady who was boldly trotting along in front of him on a Neapolitan horse worth a hundred pistoles. Everything about her clothes and the horse's caparison glittered with pearls and precious stones – the stirrups, the mountings, the buckles and rings; the curb bit and cheek piece were of pure gold and its horseshoes of the finest silver. She herself looked quite magnificent and determined, her face was like a rose in bloom, or at least looked as if she were half drunk, since she was so bright and lively in all her movements and gestures; all around her there was such a strong smell of powder, balsam, musk, ambergris and other perfumes that if it had been any other woman one would have thought she was sexually aroused. In short, everything about her was so sumptuous I would have taken her for a mighty queen if only she had been wearing a crown; and that she must be, for people said that she alone ruled over money, not money over her. Therefore at first I was surprised that the aforementioned miserable wretch on the wolf dared to speak out against her, but he was bolder than I had given him credit for.

Chapter 4

Then he forced his way through to Lucifer himself and said, "O mighty prince, there is hardly anyone on the whole of the earth whom I loathe more than this bitch, who appears to mankind in the pose of Liberality in order, with the aid of Pride, Gluttony and Lust, to bring me into disrepute and oppress me. She gets everywhere, like chaff in a manger, putting obstacles in my way as I go about my business and pulling down everything I've built up with my hard work to make your empire prosper. Is it not well-known throughout the infernal empire that men call me the root of all evil? But what joy or honour can I have in such a magnificent title if this young snotty-nosed wench is to be preferred to me? Must I – one of your most long-serving counsellors who has ever promoted your state and its infernal interests – must I, I say I! I! in my old age give way to this minx born, I assume, of Pride and Lust? No, no, a thousand times no! O mighty prince, would it become your dignity or correspond to your aim of tormenting mankind both here and there to grant that this fashion-mad little missy is right in her action against me? I must admit, however, that 'right' was a slip of the tongue, for me right and wrong are just the same. What I meant was that it would result in a reduction of your power if the industry, which I have put at your service so untiringly from time immemorial to the present day, were to be rewarded with such disdain; the repute and esteem I enjoy among mankind would be diminished and ultimately I would thus lose my place in their hearts and minds; I therefore beg that you order this ignorant young vagrant to give way to me as her elder, not to disrupt my undertakings and to allow me to continue to further your affairs of state exactly as I did previously, when no one in the whole world knew anything of her."

Once Greed, after adding even more comments, had finished, Extravagance replied that nothing surprised her more than that her grandfather should have the audacity to rage against his own family as did Herod to his relations. "He calls me," she said, "a bitch. It is true that that appellation is appropriate in so far as I am his granddaughter, but in no way can it be applied to my personal qualities. He accuses me of sometimes posing as Liberality and going about my business under that pretence – oh, the simple-minded allegation of an old ninny that arouses ridicule of himself rather than condemnation of my behaviour. Does the old fool not know that there is not one of the infernal spirits who, given the nature of their business and the demands of necessity, has not disguised themself as an angel of light? My honourable forebear should take a look at himself: has he never knocked on a person's door to seek lodgings for the night, telling them he is Thrift? Should I reproach him for that or even take him to court? No, not at all, I don't even hold it against him. We all have to use such ploys and ruses until we have slipped in unnoticed and gained access to people. I would like to hear what an honest, devout person – for they are the only ones we have to hoodwink, the godless won't escape us anyway – would say if one of us came and said, 'I am Greed, I want to take you to Hell; I am Extravagance, I want to ruin you; I am Envy follow me and you will be damned for all eternity; I am Pride, let me in and I will make you as the Devil whom God banished from his countenance, I am this or that, if you copy me you will repent it far too late, for then you will never be able to escape eternal torment.' "

"Do you not think, mighty Prince," she said to Lucifer, "that such a person would say, 'In the name of God begone, take yourself off to the abyss of Hell, down to your grandfather who sent you here, and leave me in peace.'?"

Then she said, turning to the whole company, "Is there any among you who has not been dismissed in that way if they were bold enough to approach a person with the truth, which is hated everywhere anyway? Must I then be the only fool to be burdened with the truth? And not allowed to follow our mutual grandfather, whose greatest secret weapon is the lie?

"And it sounds just as weak when the old skinflint tries to belittle me by saying Pride and Lust help me. And, anyway, if they do that they are only doing what their duty and the increase of the hellish Empire demands. But it does surprise me that he begrudges me those things he himself cannot do without. Do the records of Hell not report that those two crept into the heart of many a poor soul and prepared the way for Greed before he – Greed – even thought of being so bold as to attack such a person? You only have to check to see that those seduced by Greed were either first of all persuaded by Pride that they must have something before they can show themselves off in all their glory or that the urging of Lust persuades them that they must build up a hoard before they can enjoy the delights of lechery. Why then does my fine grandfather not want those to help me who have done him such good service?

"And as far as Intemperance and Gluttony are concerned, I can't help it if Greed keeps his subjects on such a tight rein that they can't attend to their affairs as well as mine. I keep them at it because that concerns my business and he doesn't allow them to refuse to do his bidding as long as it isn't too much for them; and I'm not claiming he's doing something illogical in that, since it is an old tradition in our infernal kingdom that every member gives the others a helping hand and we should be linked to each other like a chain. As for my ancestor's claim that he has always and everywhere been called the root of all evil and that I deliberately want to reduce him, or even be preferred to him, by my behaviour, my answer is that I neither begrudge him his well-earned reputation nor am I trying to rob him of it. But no one among the infernal spirits will blame me for trying to outdo my grandfather with my own qualities or at least to be his equal. Indeed, this would be more to his honour than to his shame, since I acknowledge that I have my origin in him. It is true that as far as my origins are concerned he has put something wrong in circulation, since he is ashamed of me because I am not, as he claims, the daughter of Lust, but in fact of his son, Excess, who begat me with Pride, the eldest daughter of the most almighty prince, at the same time as he begat Lust with Folly.

"So given that I am as noble as Mammon as far as my family background is concerned, I believe I am more useful through my qualities (though I don't seem to be quite as clever as him) than that old dodderer, and I do not intend to give way to him, let alone let him take precedence. I am quite convinced that the Grand Prince and the whole infernal army will agree with me and insist that he withdraw his insult to me, in future let me carry on my work unmolested and allow that I am of high degree and one of the most noble members of the infernal kingdom."

"Who would not be hurt," Greed on his wolf replied, "to engender such obnoxious children who are so degenerate they don't seem to belong to their family? And I am supposed to crawl away and hold my tongue when this baggage not only does everything she can to oppose me but beyond that refuses to recognise my great age and imagines she can rise above me?"

"O old man," Extravagance replied, "I am sure there must have been fathers who have had a child that was better than they."

"But more often," Mammon replied, "there have been parents who have had to complain about their undutiful children."

"What's the point of all this quarrelling?" Lucifer said. "Let each one show what they do for the good of our kingdom and we will judge which one of you deserves precedence. And in making our judgment we will take neither age nor youth, nor sex nor anything else into account; for the one who is found to be most abhorrent to the great Deity and of most harm to human beings will, following our immemorial custom, also be cock of the roost here."

"As I am, o great prince, now permitted to present my great qualities and in how many ways I render exceptional services to the infernal state through them," Mammon replied, "then I do not doubt that, if I describe them well enough in detail and others listen to me properly, the whole infernal kingdom will acknowledge my superiority over Extravagance. In addition, they will ascribe to me the honour and seat of old departed Pluto, under which name I was formerly respected as the supreme sovereign, that rank being my due. I am not going to boast that humans themselves call me the root of all evil, that is a spring, a cloaca, a morass as they call everything that is harmful to both their bodies and souls, and can, by contrast, be of advantage to our infernal kingdom. All this is so well known that even children are familiar with it!

"Nor am I going to go on about how those who are followers of the great Deity daily vilify me and revile me like flat beer in order to make me hated by all humans. And yet it is no small honour for me that, despite all such persecution inspired by the Deity, I still manage to find access to humans, set up a fixed abode there and maintain it, despite all the storm winds blowing. And is it not to my honour that I command all those to whom the Deity gave the honest warning that they could not serve me and him at the same time and that under me his words are like the good seeds that fell among thorns and choked?

"However I am going to remain silent about all this because, as I said, they are old tricks that are all too well-known already! But there is one thing, just one thing I will boast of and that is that none of all the spirits and members of the infernal kingdom realise the intentions of our great prince better than I; for his desire and determination is that humans should not have a quiet, pleasant and peaceful life down below, nor have and enjoy bliss in eternity.

"Just look at all the nasty surprises they get, the way those people set about things and then struggle – people to whom I have only little access; then the constant fear of those who start to let me into their hearts; and just have a little look at the life of those whom I hold in complete possession and then tell me whether there is a more wretched creature on earth or whether any single infernal spirit has taken over and finished off a greater or more steadfast martyr than the ones I draw into our empire? I constantly rob him of his sleep, that his own nature seriously demands from him; and even if he is compelled by his need to rest, I so tease and torment him with all kinds of worrying and troublesome dreams, that he not only cannot find rest but sins more in his sleep than some do when awake.

"I keep those who are comfortably off on shorter commons as far as food and drink and other fare are concerned, than the poorest enjoy. And if I didn't now and then shut my eyes as a favour to Pride, they would have to wear even more ragged clothes than the poorest of the poor. I allow them no joy, no rest, no peace, no pleasure, in fact nothing people call good and would allow their bodies, never mind their souls, to flourish, yes, I even go so far as not to allow them that lust which other children of the word seek and thus fall to us; I even lace their carnal desires, to which all on earth are by their very nature addicted, with bitterness by coupling radiant youths with old, decrepit, horrible, barren hags, the fairest maidens with jealous greybeard cuckolds and ruining their happiness. Their greatest delight has to be to fret with worry and care, their supreme content, when they wear themselves out with hellish exertions to earn a little gold that they can't take with them.

"I don't allow them any honest prayers, even less that they give alms out of the goodness of their hearts; and if they do quite often fast or, to put it more precisely, suffer the pangs of hunger, it is not out of piety but to save something in order to please me. I put them in physical and mortal danger, not solely on ships at sea but also in the abyss beneath the waves; indeed they have to rummage through the innermost entrails of the earth for me and if there were something to be fished out of the air I would make them learn to fish. I won't mention the wars I start, nor the suffering they cause, for these things are known all over the world. Nor will I list all the usurers I create, the cutpurses, thieves, robbers and murderers, since I pride myself that all who are associated with me have to drag themselves along in bitter care, fear, privation, hardship and work; and although I punish their bodies so terribly that they need no other torturer, I also torment them in their minds, so that no other infernal spirit is needed to give them a foretaste of Hell, not to mention hold us in respect. I terrify the rich! I oppress the poor! I turn Justice blind, I drive away Christian charity, without which no one can go to Heaven. Compassion has no place with me!

Chapter 5

While Greed was rambling on praising himself and putting himself above Extravagance, one of the infernal crew came shambling along who seemed to be frail with old age, lame and hunchbacked. He was wheezing like a bear or as if he'd been chasing a rabbit, which made all those present prick up their ears to hear his news or what kind of game he'd caught, for he had the reputation of being particularly adept at that compared with other spirits. But once he came out with his story, they saw there was nothing to it and he had been prevented from carrying out his plan, for when he was granted permission to speak, they heard that he had approached Julus, a nobleman from England, and his servant Avarus, who had left their country to visit France, and tried to ensnare them in vain. He had been unable to get anywhere with the former because of his noble nature and virtuous upbringing and with the latter, on the other hand, because of his simple piety. He therefore asked Lucifer to give him more support.

That was at the point where it seemed as if Mammon had concluded his speech and Extravagance was about to begin hers. But Lucifer said, "It is not words that are needed. It is said that we are known by our works and so each of you two

32

adversaries is hereby given the task of taking one of these Englishmen in hand, of attacking, tempting and challenging him until one or the other of you has caught your victim in your snares, bound him, and made him part of our infernal kingdom. And whichever of you brings him here most certainly and securely will win the prize and enjoy ascendancy over the other."

All the infernal spirits praised this decision and the two who were in dispute came to an agreement, on the suggestion of Pride, that Mammon should take Julus in hand and Extravagance Avarus. They did this with the express proviso that neither of them should take the least action to harm the other's chances with their victim unless the interest of the infernal kingdom expressly demanded it.

At that it was marvellous to behold how the other vices wished both of them the best of luck and offered to accompany, help and serve them. With that the whole infernal gathering broke up, at which a strong wind arose which sent me, together with Extravagance and Greed and their followers and supporters, in a trice to a place between England and France and deposited us all on the very ship on which the two Englishmen had crossed the Channel and were about to disembark.

Pride went straight up to Julus and said, "O bold cavalier, I am Repute and, since you are about to enter a foreign country, it would suit me very well if you were to make me your major-domo. Here you can show the inhabitants, through special elegance, that you are not a poor nobleman but come from the line of the old kings. And even if that is not the case, you would still be able to show the French, to the honour of your nation, what valiant men England possesses."

At this Julus got his servant Avarus to pay the ship's owner for the journey in pure though coarse, but still fair and lovely gold coins, at which the owner made Julus a humble bow and several times called him his most gracious lord. Pride exploited this and said to Avarus, "See how a person is honoured when they harbour such fellows." Greed, however, said to him, "If you had so many of these residing with you, you would have invested them in a different way. For it is much better for the supply and abundance to be invested at a certain interest, so that in future you will be able to enjoy some of it, than to throw it away to no effect on a journey that is full of pain, worry and danger anyway."

Hardly had the two young men stepped onto dry land than Arrogance was quietly assuring Extravagance that at her first knocking at the door she had not only acquired entry but, so it seemed, a permanent seat in Julus' heart, adding that she wanted to gather further assistance from outside so that she could pursue her project all the more surely. She was, she said, not going to be far from Extravagance but all the same she had to give the same help to her opponent, Greed, as she, Extravagance could expect from her.

If I had a story to tell, Gracious reader, I would be brief and not go on at such length. I have to admit that I demand that any storyteller should not keep people waiting for a long time. But what I am recounting here is a vision or dream, that is something very different. I must not rush on to the end but bring in certain minor details and situations so that I can tell a more complete story, which I intend to present to the people here. That is nothing other than to give an example of how a little spark can turn into a great fire, if one does not take care. For just as it is rare for someone in this world to reach the highest degree of holiness all at once, similarly no one turns in the blink of an eye from a devout man into a rogue, but each goes his way gradually, step by step. I therefore feel justified in not omitting any stage in the road to ruin, so that everyone can learn to avoid them in time, and to that end I mostly describe those in which our two young men were like young deer seeing the huntsman and at first not knowing whether to flee or to stay, and are therefore shot before they realise what the huntsman is doing. They did fall into the trap rather more quickly than is usual, but the reason was that in each the tinder was ready to ignite from the sparks of this or that vice. Just as young cattle, when they have been through the winter and are released from the tedious barn into the enticing meadow, start to romp, even though they might jump into a crevice or fence-post to their own undoing, so it is with thoughtless youths when they are no longer under the restraint of paternal discipline, when they are out of their parents' sight, enjoying their long-awaited freedom – and usually lack experience and caution.

Pride was not making the comments to Extravagance quoted above simply to pass the time, but immediately went to work and turned to Avarus only to find Envy and Resentment there already. Greed had sent these two comrades to prepare the way for him and with this in mind they turned to the servant and said, "Listen, Avarus, are you not just as much of a man as your master? Are you not just as much of an Englishman as Julus? How comes it, then, that people call him your lord and master and you his lackey? Has England not given birth to both of you and nurtured you? Why is it that here in this country, where he has as little that belongs to him as you, he is treated as a noble lord and you as his slave? Did you both not come here across the sea? And could he not have drowned just as well as you if you had been shipwrecked on the way? Or would he, being of noble blood, have escaped the storms under the waves, like a dolphin, and reached a safe harbour? Or could he perhaps have risen like an eagle above the clouds, which were the origin and cause of your shipwreck, and thus avoid destruction? No, Avarus, Julus is just as much of a man as you and you are just as much of a man as he. Then why should he be placed so far above you?"

At that Mammon interrupted Pride and said, "Is that the way to go about it, to encourage someone to fly before they have grown feathers? As if it wasn't well-known that it is money that makes Julus what he is! It's his money, his money, that makes him what he is, otherwise he's nothing, nothing, I say, apart from what his money makes him. Let the good fellow wait just a little while and let me have my way and see if I can't make Avarus, through hard work and obedience, get as much money as Julus squanders and by that make him into such a dandy as Julus already is."

Thus the initial temptation of Avarus came from a figure to whom he not only listened to avidly but also decided to follow; nor did Julus desist from diligently putting into practice everything Pride suggested to him.

Chapter 6

The lord and master, that is Mr Julus, spent the night in the place where we had landed and stayed there the next day and the following night in order to rest, to collect his bills of exchange and to make arrangements to travel on through the Spanish Netherlands to Holland. He not only desired to visit the United Provinces but had been expressly ordered to do so by his father. For this purpose he hired a bizarre carriage, just for himself and his servant Avarus; however, Pride and Extravagance, together with Greed and all their train had no intention of being left behind and each sat wherever they could find room, Pride up on the roof, Extravagance beside Julus, Greed in Avarus' heart – and I squatted on the boot at the back, since Modesty wasn't there to take that place.

Thus I had the good fortune to view in my dream many fine cities that hardly one person in a thousand would see while awake. The journey went well and, although there were some dangerous incidents, Julus' well-filled coffers overcame them all, for he gave freely of his money and used it to procure the necessary passes and safe conducts because we had to pass through territory guarded by various hostile garrisons. I didn't particularly concern myself with the things that are generally regarded as worth seeing in these lands but observed how the two young men came more and more under the influence of the above-mentioned vices.

More joined them the longer the journey continued, and I saw how Julus was attacked and captured by Presumption and Unchastity (which is accused of being a sin with which Pride is punished). As a result we often had to spend more time waiting in places where there were loose women and squandered more money than our needs would normally require. Avarus, on the other hand, made every effort to accumulate as much money as he could, not only stealing from his master but our landlords and hosts, wherever we went. He even made an excellent pimp and showed no hesitation in purloining things from the people who gave us lodgings, even if it was just a silver spoon.

Thus we made our way through Flanders, Brabant, Hainault, Holland, Zealand, Zutphen, Geldern, Mechelen, then across the border to France and eventually to Paris, where Julus took the most comfortable and pleasant lodgings he could find. He dressed his Avarus as a noble squire, so that everyone would think he himself was of higher standing because he had a man of rank as his servant, calling him 'My Lord' – eventually he was assumed to be a Count. He took a lutenist, a swordsman, a dancing master and a tennis coach into his service, more for the sake of show than to learn their skills. These were all the kind of fellows who were masters at fleecing young men who had just left home. They soon made him acquainted with wenches with whom nothing was to be had without spending money and introduced him to all kinds of company where he had to foot the bill, and pay through the nose at that. For Extravagance had already invited Lust with all his daughters, to help to attack this Julus and bring about his downfall.

At first he contented himself with playing at the ball and tilting at the ring, with plays, ballets and similar legitimate and honourable exercises, which he attended and joined in himself. Once he had become enthusiastic and well-known, however, he was also taken to places where people were after his money with cards and dice, until eventually he was making merry in the most expensive whorehouses.

In his lodgings, however, it was like the court of King Arthur. Every day he was surrounded by parasites and he didn't fob them off them with cabbage and turnips but set expensive French potages and Spanish *olla potrida* before them; thus a single meal could cost him over twenty-five pistoles, especially if you included the musicians he generally got to play there. As well as that, the new fashions in clothes cost him dear as they changed so quickly and he indulged in this foolishness all the more because, as a foreign gentleman no dress was forbidden him; it all had to be embroidered and trimmed with gold and not a month passed when he didn't put on a new outfit, nor a day when he didn't powder his wig several times. Although he had naturally beautiful hair, Pride persuaded him to have it cut off and to adorn himself with that of others because that was the custom – for people would say that those eccentrics who kept their own hair, however beautiful it was, were thus telling people that they were poor wretches who couldn't afford to pay a paltry hundred ducats for a couple of wigs. In brief: everything Pride thought up had to be as expensive as Extravagance could make it.

Although such a style of life was repulsive to Greed, who already had Avarus entirely in his clutches, Avarus made it seem attractive to him, for he intended to make use of it. Mammon had already encouraged him to follow Disloyalty, if he wanted prosper himself. Thus he seized every opportunity to steal as much as he could from his master, who was throwing his money away anyway; the least he did was not to pay any seamstress or washerwoman without reducing their normal wages and putting what he took from them in his own pocket; no payment for repairing clothes or polishing shoes was too small for him to exaggerate it and keep the extra for himself, not to mention the way he siphoned off as much as he could by any means from greater expenses; and the men who carried his master in his sedan chair soon found they'd been replaced, if they didn't pass on part of their earnings to him; the pastry cook, the chef, the vintner, the wood-dealer, baker and other suppliers of food had to share their profits with him if they wanted to keep such a good customer as Julus. For Avarus was taken with the idea of equalling his master in the amount of money and goods he possessed, just as Lucifer had been emboldened by the gifts granted him by the Lord as to place his seat beside the throne of Almighty God.

Thus the two young men lived on without a care in the world, until they realised in what way they were living. For Julus was as rich in worldly goods as Avarus was lacking in them, and both assumed they were behaving in a way appropriate to their status, that is as everyone's social status and circumstances demand. It was right for Julus to appear in splendour that corresponded to his wealth and for Avarus to exploit the present opportunity his spendthrift master provided to do something about his poverty and feather his own nest. Nevertheless that inner watchman, the light of reason that never remains silent, namely our conscience, was constantly reproaching each of them for their mistakes and telling them to think again.

"Go easy now, go easy," it said to Julus. "Stop squandering what your ancestors earned by the sweat of their brow, yes, perhaps even with the loss of their salvation, and thoughtfully saved up for you; invest it instead, so that in future you can face your God, the reputable world and your descendants and account for what you have done," etc. But the reply to these salutary reminders, trying to persuade Julus to moderate his way of life, was, "I'm not a miserable stay-at-home, nor a penny-pinching Jew, I'm a cavalier! Should I follow my noble pursuits in the form of a miserable beggar or knave? No, that is not the custom nor the tradition, I'm not here to suffer hunger and thirst, even less to scrimp and save like some miserly old Jew, but to live on my income like an honest fellow." And when the good ideas, that he was in the habit of calling melancholy thoughts, still kept on exhorting him to mend his ways, his response was the same old song, "Let us enjoy the day while it lasts, God knows where we'll be tomorrow," or he'd go to see a whore or some merry company with whom he could get drunk. And the longer it went on, the worse it became until eventually he was an out-and-out hedonist.

Avarus too was told by inner voices that the road he was setting out on to acquire wealth was the greatest breach of trust in the world. He was further reminded that he had been appointed not merely to serve his master, but to prevent him from suffering loss, to promote his welfare, to encourage him in all honest virtues and to warn him against shameful vices; and above all he was to be industrious in keeping his worldly goods together and guarding them.

But, on the contrary, he was grasping these for himself and encouraging Julus to fall prey to all kinds of vices. How did he think he could justify his actions – before God, to whom he had to account for everything; before Julus' devout parents, who had entrusted their only son to him and commanded him to keep watch over him faithfully; and, finally, before Julus himself when the day should come, sooner or later, when he realised that through his neglect and infidelity he had been personally depraved and his wealth squandered to no effect whatsoever.

"And that is not all, o Avarus, for with this heavy responsibility with which you are burdening yourself for Julus' person and money, you are sullying yourself with the shameful vice of theft and are worthy of the gallows; you are subjecting your eternal soul to the mire of worldly goods, which you intend to gather together in a disloyal and criminal way – which even a heathen such as Crates Thebanus threw into the sea so that they would not defile him, despite the fact that they were rightfully his. In your case you can expect them to bring about your downfall, as you, on the other hand, try to fish them out of the great ocean of your disloyalty! Do you imagine they will bring you good fortune?"

Avarus did hear such exhortations from his own good sense and conscience, but he had no lack of excuses to gloss over the evil course he had set out upon. "What?" he said about Julus, referring to Proverbs 26, "what is the point of honour, money and a good life for a fool? They are not seemly for him – moreover he has more than enough. And who knows how his parents came about them? Is it not better that I should grasp for myself those things that he will squander without me and let them go to strangers anyway?"

Thus the two young men continued blindly on their way, drowning in the bottomless pit of their desires, until finally Julus caught the French disease and had to sweat it out for a week or four, purging both his body and his purse, though this did not make him any better, nor serve as a warning, illustrating the truth of the common saying, 'Once the sick man got better, the worse he was.'

Chapter 7

Avarus stole so much money it frightened him, especially since he didn't know what to do with it so that Julus wouldn't find out about his thieving. So he thought up a clever plan to avert any suspicion. He changed all his gold into heavy silver German coins, put them all in a large knapsack and came running up to his master's bedroom at night with a lie or, to put it more politely, a story about what a find he'd made.

"Master," he said, "I stumbled over this when some men threw me out of your mistress' apartment and if the metal hadn't made a different sound from the entrails of a corpse, I would have thought I'd tripped over a dead man!"

With that he emptied out the money and went on, "What advice would your Lordship give me about how to return this money to its rightful owner? I would hope he would give me a goodly tip out of it."

"Don't be a fool," Julius replied, "if you've got something, keep it. Now tell me what reply you have from the lady?"

"I didn't manage to get to speak to her this evening," Avarus replied, "because, as I said, there were some men threatening me and I had to run off, which was when I happened across this money."

Thus Avarus lied his head off, as many young thieves do, when they pretend to have found the things they have stolen.

Just at that time Julus received letters from his father which included a strong reproach for his dissolute way of life and for being such a spendthrift – the English merchants with whom he corresponded and who paid Julus his allowance had told him everything about Julus and Avarus' behaviour, apart from the fact that his servant was stealing from him without him noticing. He was so distressed by this that he fell seriously ill and wrote to the merchants that from now on they should only give his son enough for the bare necessities an ordinary nobleman needed to get by in Paris, adding that if they gave his son more he would not reimburse them for it. As for Julus, he threatened that if he did not mend his ways he would even disinherit him and no longer regard him as his son.

Julus was very dismayed by this but still did not resolve to live more frugally, for if he had tried to do as his father insisted and avoided great expenditure, that would have been impossible because he was already far too deep in debt. He would have lost all credit with his creditors and, as a result, with everyone else, which Pride advised strongly against because it would ruin his reputation, which he had gained by being lavish with his money. Therefore he said to his countrymen, "You gentlemen know that my father not only has shares in many ships, that sail to the West and East Indies, but on his estate at home has between four and five thousand sheep that are sheared every year, so that no gentleman in the country is his equal and certainly not greater than him. And that is without mentioning the cash and land he possesses!

"You also know," he went on, "that I am the sole heir to

his whole fortune, which I will inherit in the near future, since my father is close to his end. And that being the case, who would expect me to idle away my time here? If I were to do that, would it not bring shame on our entire nation? I beg you, gentlemen, do not let me suffer that disgrace; help me, as you have done so far, by advancing me some money which I will pay back with gratitude and, until that day, add interest at the standard rate; and I will show each one of you such respect that you will be content with me."

At this some just shrugged their shoulders and made their excuses, saying that at the moment they had no money to spare; in fact they were honest men and didn't want to anger Julus' father. The others, however, were thinking how they could fleece Julus if they could just get him in their claws. "Who knows how long the old man will go on living," they said to themselves, "and a man who saves needs a spendthrift anyway; even if his father does disinherit him, he can't take his inheritance from his mother away from him." All in all these men advanced Julus another one thousand ducats in return for which he pledged them whatever they asked for and promised them eight per cent annual interest, all of which was then written down in the appropriate terms.

Julus didn't get very far with that, for by the time he'd paid his debts and Avarus had sliced off his share, there wasn't much left, with the result that he soon had to take out more loans and give more pledges. Other Englishmen, who were not involved in this, quickly informed his father. He was so angry with those who had lent his son money against his orders, that he took legal steps against them and also, reminding them of his previous letter, told them he would not reimburse them for one single penny and, what was more, if they should come back to England, he would indict them in parliament as corrupters of young men. To Julus he sent a letter in his own hand saying that he should no longer call himself his son, nor show his face at home again.

When this news came things started to go badly for Julus again. He still had some money, but far too little either to continue in his extravagant ways or to equip himself for a journey and serve some lord in the wars with a pair of horses, to which both Pride and Extravagance encouraged him. And since no one was willing to advance him anything for this, he begged his loyal servant Avarus to lend him some of the money he had found. To this Avarus replied, "Your Lordship knows what a poor soul I was and have nothing but that which God recently gave to me."

(Oh, you hypocritical rogue, I thought, did God give you all that money you stole from your master? In his hour of need should you not come to his aid with his own money? And that all the more because as long as he had money you joined in and played your part in throwing his money away on food and drink, whores, knaves, gambling and banquets? O you wretch, I thought, you did come from England as a sheep, but since Greed has had you in his power you have become a fox, nay, even a wolf in France.)

"If now," he went on, "I did not look after those gifts from God and invest them to support my future life, I would be afraid that I would show myself to be unworthy of all the future happiness that I have to look forward to. Any man who receives a blessing from God, should thank Him, and for the rest of my life I am unlikely to make another such find.

Should I now put this in a place where even rich Englishmen refuse to make any more loans, because they already have the best pledge in their hands, who would advise me to do that? Moreover did not Your Lordship yourself tell me that if I had something, I should keep it? And, anyway, all my money is in the exchange bank, and I cannot take it out at will without denying myself a high level of interest."

Julus found it difficult to swallow all this; it was the kind of thing he was not used to hearing from his faithful servant, nor from other people. But Pride and Extravagance had him so much in their power that he easily got over it and accepted it. Then, by pleading, he brought Avarus to the point where he agreed to lend him all the money he had stolen or siphoned off, on condition that his wages and what they might incur in the way of four weeks' interest, would be added to the sum bearing interest at eight per cent per annum; and, to secure the loan and interest, a noble estate Julus had inherited from his mother's sister was to be mortgaged to him. All of this was immediately drawn up in the correct form, with the other Englishmen as witnesses; the total sum came to six hundred pounds sterling which, when converted into our currency, was a goodly sum of money.

Hardly had the above contract been drawn up and signed, than Julus received the announcement of some sad news that pleased him well, namely that his father had gone the way of all flesh. At this he immediately put on princely mourning and prepared to travel to England as soon as possible, more to take up his inheritance than to comfort his mother. Then, to my surprise, I saw that Julus once more had a crowd of friends he had not had a few days previously. I also saw how he could play the hypocrite: when he was among people, he pretended he was sorry for his father; but when alone with Avarus, he said, "If the old man had stayed alive much longer, I would eventually have had to go home begging, especially if you had not come to my help with your money."

Chapter 8

Then Julus, having dismissed his other servants – lackeys, pages and suchlike useless, gluttonous, wasteful people – with a decent reward, quickly set off with Avarus. If I wanted to see how this story ended, I had to accompany them, of course, but we undertook the journey in varying degrees of comfort. Julus was on a splendid stallion, because the one thing he had learnt was how to ride, and sitting behind him, as if she were his bride or lover, was Extravagance. Avarus was on a gelding with Greed behind him, looking like some pedlar or mountebank riding to a fair with his monkey. Pride, on the other hand, was flying high in the air as if the journey did not particularly concern her. The other vices present walked along beside them, as footboys do, but I grabbed hold of a horse's tail here and there, so that I could accompany them and see England. I had already seen many countries but I imagined this land would be something unusual. We soon reached the town with the landing stage, where we had previously disembarked, and in a short time were sailing with a good wind.

When he arrived home Julus found his mother at death's door as well, and she departed this life that very same day, so that he was now of age and sole heir and master of all his parents had left him. And now the good life started again, even better than in Paris, for he had inherited a considerable sum in cash. He lived like the rich man in the Gospel of St Luke, chapter 16, even like a prince, now with guests, now invited by others; almost daily he went for excursions on land or water with other people's daughters or wives, as is the English custom, had his own trumpeter, riding master, valet, buffoon, groom, coachman, two lackeys, a page, huntsman, cook and suchlike court servants. He treated all of these in a very benign fashion, especially Avarus, who, as his faithful companion on his journey, he had made his majordomo and steward. Then he also made over to Avarus the estate he had previously mortgaged to him in France in return for his loan, the interest and his wages, even though it was worth much more. In short, he behaved in such a way to everyone that I not only thought he must be descended from the old kings, as he had often boasted in France, but was convinced he must come from the line of King Arthur, the praise of whose generosity will sound until the end of the world.

Avarus, for his part, continued to fish in these waters whenever he saw a chance. He stole more than ever from his master and haggled worse than a fifty-year-old Jew. The worst trick he played on Julus was that he had an affair with a woman from an honourable family, then passed her on to his master and, nine months later, got him to acknowledge the child he had given her as his own. Since Julus could not bring himself to marry this woman, even though that meant he would be in danger from her friends, honest Avarus came to his rescue and allowed himself to be persuaded to restore her honour, even though he had enjoyed her favours more than Julus and was himself the cause of her downfall. Through this he once more took a further part of Julus' wealth to himself and through this show of loyalty stood even higher in his master's esteem. Yet he continued to fleece him as long as there was anything he could get his hands on, however little it was.

Once Julus made a boating trip on the Thames with his closest relatives, among whom was his father's brother, a very wise and sensible man, who on that occasion had a more intimate conversation with him than usual. Speaking politely and with mild reproach, he pointed out to him that he was not very thrifty and that he ought to take better care of his estate and his fortune etc. If youth only knew the needs of old age, he said, they would turn a ducat over a hundred times before spending it. Julus laughed at this, took a ring off his finger and threw it in the Thames, saying, "Uncle, I am no more likely to squander all my wealth than I am to get that ring back."

The old man sighed replying, "Go easy, nephew, even a king's fortune can be squandered and a spring run dry. Just be careful what you do." But Julus turned away from him, hating him even more for his well-meant warning than he should have loved him for it.

Not long afterwards some merchants came from France and, having heard about Julus' way of life and that a richly laden ship his parents had sent to Alexandria had been taken by pirates on the Mediterranean, wanted the principal they had lent him paid back, together with the interest.

He paid them with jewels, which was an indication that he was running out of ready money. As well as that there came news that another of his ships had sunk on the shore of Brazil and that part of an English fleet, in which his parents had invested heavily, had been wrecked by the Dutch not far from the Moluccas and the rest captured.

All of this soon became widely known and anyone who had some claim to make of Julus demanded payment, so that it looked as if misfortune were coming upon him from all the corners of the world. But all these disasters frightened him less than his cook, who showed him a gold ring he had found in a fish, for he recognised it as his own and remembered what he had said as he threw it in the river.

He was quite depressed, almost desperate, but was ashamed to let people see how he felt. Just then he heard that the executed king's eldest prince had landed in Scotland with an army and, after some success, had good prospects of winning back his father's kingdom. Julus thought he could take advantage of this to restore his reputation, so he used what money was left to him to equip himself and his men, making a fine cavalry cohort, of which he appointed Avarus lieutenant, promising him the moon if he would accompany him. All of this was on the pretext of helping the Lord Protector; however, when he had his cohort together, he took his company at a forced march to join up with the army of the young Scottish king. This would have been good if the king had been successful, but when Cromwell destroyed his army, Julus and Avarus just managed to escape with their lives, but could not show their faces anywhere. They were forced to live in the woods like wild animals, and feed themselves by robbing and stealing, until they were finally caught and executed, Julus with the axe and Avarus on the gallows, which he had long deserved.

At this I came back to myself, or at least woke from my sleep and reflected on my dream or story, coming to the conclusion that liberality can easily lead to extravagance and parsimony to greed, if a person lacks the sense to keep their liberality and parsimony within bounds. Whether Greed or Extravagance won the contest I cannot say; in fact, I am sure that they are still daily fighting in their efforts to come out on top.

Chapter 9

One day I was walking in the woods, listening to my idle thoughts, when I came across a life-size stone figure lying on the ground. It looked as if it was the statue of some ancient German hero, for it had old-fashioned clothes like a Roman soldier's uniform with a large bib over its chest. To me it seemed very skilfully carved and looked very natural. As I stood there looking at it and wondering how it came to be out there in the wilderness, it occurred to me that long ago there must have been a heathen temple on that hill and this would have been the idol in it. I therefore looked round to see if there was something of its foundations left but I saw nothing. However, since I found a lever some lumberjack must have left there, I took it and tried to turn the statue over to see what it was like on the other side. But hardly had I placed the lever under its neck, than it started to move, saying, "Leave me in peace, I am Soon-Another."

That gave me a start, but I recovered at once and said, "I can well see that you are soon another. At first you were just a dead stone and now you're a moving body. But who else can you be, the devil or his mother?"

"No," it replied, "I am neither of those but Soon-Another,

as you yourself called me and recognised me as such. And how could it be possible that you wouldn't know me, since I have been with you all the days of your life? However, I have never talked to you, as I did on the last day of July 1534 to Hans Sachs, the cobbler of Nuremberg, and that is the reason why you have never noticed me, despite the fact that I have made you now big, now small, now rich, now poor, now up, now down, now happy, now sad, now bad, now good – all in all, now one way and soon another."

"If you can do nothing apart from that," I said, "then it would have been better if you had stayed away from me this time as well."

Soon-Another replied, "Since my origin is in paradise and my nature and activities will continue as long as the world lasts, I will never leave you until you return to the earth from which you are formed, whether you like it or not."

I asked him whether he was of no other use to people than to change them and all their actions in so many different ways?

"O yes," Soon-Another replied, "I can teach them an art by which they can talk to all objects that are by their nature mute, to chairs and benches for example, to pots and pans etc. I taught Hans Sachs how to do this and he then recorded in his book two such conversations he had, with a ducat and a horse's skin."

"O my dear Soon-Another," I said, "if, with God's help, you could teach me that art as well I would love you all my days."

"Indeed I will," he replied. Then he took my book, that I happened to have with me, and wrote the following in it:

"I am the beginning and the end, my rule obtains in

all places.

"Ymbro urknic avvilin, irbnim Agolg istnin eproy oncrnu raasles, entrl fazzow; hanba thoich amas harza perp erkven erolid, Tozzero eulliv erouzr yaoht hilleti nylag arvan daum. Adjuk encres plexe ervic hoyjo, uxt oltilf inixt; Ardovn dandrab entivel iridie, vereste wah ambdt iss liverdi, kxqe tulzer ulthut harrada neqid. Yourvo umow indixil luh axiv empew hacra tyshy, Omplu ravvif oppo lzti sallah flopera nuc yorow araxan tizlits."[1]

Once he had written this he turned into a great oak tree, then into a pig, quickly into a fried sausage and, before I could grab it, into a large turd (with your permission); he then became a fair meadow of clover and, before I knew what was happening, into a cowpat; then into a beautiful flower or twig, into a mulberry tree and after that into a splendid silk carpet etc, until he finally changed back into human form, frequently changing that too, as the aforementioned Hans Sachs described. Since I had never read about such a variety of rapid metamorphoses, neither in Ovid nor anywhere else (for at that time I had not yet seen Hans Sachs), I thought that Proteus must have risen from the dead to mock me with his tricks, or that it was the devil himself, come to tempt and deceive me as a hermit. However, after he had told me that he bore the moon in his coat of arms with more right than the Turkish emperor, that Inconstancy was where he lived and Constancy his worst enemy, though he didn't care a fig for that, since he had several times driven her away, he changed himself into a bird and flew off, leaving me standing there.

---

1 Take out the first and last letter of each word and run them together to get the sense of this.

The Continuation of Simplicissimus

So I sat down in the grass and started to look at the words Soon-Another had left me to see if I could learn the art from them. However, I didn't have the heart to say them out loud, for they were so strange, un-German and incomprehensible that they seemed to me like those satanists use to conjure up evil spirits and perform other magic spells.

"If you start to say them," I said to myself, "who knows what demons you will attract. Perhaps this Soon-Another is Satan who wants to use them to seduce you. Don't you remember what happened to the old hermits?"

However, I couldn't stop myself continuing to look at the words he had written, because I would have liked to be able to talk to mute things, especially as others are said to have been able to understand the dumb animals. The longer I thought about it, the keener I became and since, without wanting to boast, I can say that I am quite good at deciphering things and the least of my accomplishments is to write a letter on a thread or even on a hair, which no one would be able to work out or guess; and long ago I solved other cryptic writings as for example Trithemius' steganography. So then I looked anew at these words and saw that in what he had written Soon-Another had told me about the art in good German words more clearly than I would have expected from him. I was very content with that and didn't pay much attention to my new knowledge, but went home and read the legends of the old saints, not just for the spiritual edification I would gain from them in my solitary life but also to help to pass the time.

Chapter 10

The life of St Alexis was the first to catch my eye when I opened the book. There I saw his contempt for idleness that made him leave his wealthy father's house, visit the holy places several times with great devotion and end both his pilgrimage and his life in extreme poverty, incomparable patience and remarkable constancy beneath the stairs of the house where some Christians had taken him in.

"O Simplicius," I said to myself, "what are you doing? You are living in idleness, serving neither God nor other people. If someone is alone, who will help them back up if they should fall? Would it not be better if you were serving your fellow men and they you, instead of sitting here in solitude like a night owl with no company whatsoever? By remaining here are you not as good as dead as a member of the human race? And then how are you going to survive the winter, when this hill is covered in snow and your neighbours can no longer bring you sustenance? At the moment they do honour you as an oracle, but once the novelty has worn off they will no longer think you worthy of even a backward glance, and instead of bringing things to you, they will send you away from their door with a 'May God help you'. Perhaps Soon-Another appeared to you personally so that you will prepare yourself in good time to accept the inconstancy of the world." I tormented myself with such thoughts and worries until I decided to leave the woods and become a pilgrim.

Accordingly I immediately picked up my scissors and shortened my long coat, which came right down to my feet – and as long as I was a hermit had served me as a mattress and blanket. The piece I had cut off I sewed on the outside and inside, as appropriate, to make pockets and a sack where I could keep the things I managed to beg off people. And since I had no nicely turned pilgrim's staff, I used the trunk of a wild apple tree with which I believed I could well knock out anyone who might come at me with a sword; later on in my pilgrimage a pious locksmith fitted a strong point to the end of my cudgel so that I could defend myself against any wolves I should happen to meet on my way.

Thus equipped, I went to Schappach in the Black Forest where I begged from the pastor there a document attesting that I had lived as a hermit not far from his parish but now intended to visit the Holy Places, even though the man told me he didn't really believe me.

"I suspect, my friend," he said, "that you have either committed some evil deed, which means you have to leave your habitation at such short notice, or you intend to be a second Empedocles Agrigentius, who threw himself into the fiery crater of Etna, so that people would believe he had been taken up into heaven because they could not find him anywhere. How would it be if one of these were the case with you and I was helping you in it with my honest testimony?"

However, with my gift of the gab and a show of pious

simplicity and honest devoutness, I managed to convince him and he gave me the document I was asking for. I sensed a holy envy or fervour in him, and that he was glad to see me go on my way because, with my unusually strict and exemplary life, the man held me in greater respect than he did some of the other clerics in the district, even though I was a disreputable customer compared with the true priests and servants of God.

At the time, though, I wasn't as ungodly as I was to become later, but would have been taken for a man of honest opinions and intentions. However, once I became acquainted with old vagabonds and the longer I went around with them and talked to them, the worse I became. Eventually you might even have called me the mentor and guild master of that company of men who make vagrancy their profession for no other purpose than to gain their sustenance from it. My clothes and figure were particularly suited to persuading people to be generous. When I came to a town, or was let into a city, especially on Sundays and feast days, I was immediately surrounded by a bigger crowd of young and old than the best huckster with his couple of fools, monkeys and meerkats. Because of my long hair and straggling beard and the fact that I always went bare-headed, whatever the weather, some saw me as one of the old prophets, others as some kind of strange miracle worker; most of them, however, took me for the Wandering Jew who must walk the earth until the Second Coming. I didn't accept money as alms, for I knew how much use to me that had been while I was a hermit; if anyone tried to force some on me, I would say, "Beggars should not have any money." The result of this was that when people saw me reject a few coppers, they gave me more food and drink than I could have bought with a few coins of a higher denomination.

Thus I walked up the Gutach and across the Black Forest to Villingen heading for Switzerland, during the course of which nothing special or unusual happened to me apart from the kind of thing I have already talked about. From there I knew the route to Einsiedeln, so didn't have to ask anyone, and once I reached Schaffhausen I was not only allowed in but, after a lot of mockery I had to suffer from the common people, I was given lodging by an honest, wealthy citizen. That happened when, as a well-travelled man who must have had many good and bad experiences on his travels, he took pity on me because some nasty lads had started throwing dung from the streets at me.

Chapter 11

My host was half drunk when he took me home and therefore wanted me to tell him where I was going, whence I came from, what my profession was and that kind of thing. He was amazed when he heard how many countries I'd been through during my life, places that not many people would see, for example, Moscow, Tartary, Persia, China, Turkey and the Antipodes and kept pressing wine from the Danube and the Tyrol on me. He himself had been to Rome, Venice, Ragusa, Constantinople and Alexandria and since I could talk about many sights and customs of such places, he believed the stories I made up about distant countries and cities, for I followed Friedrich von Logau's maxim where he says:

> If thou wouldst lie, then tell
> Stories of lands far away,
> For those who are drawn to them
> Will gladly hear what you say.

And once I had seen how successful this was, I went almost right round the world with my stories: I had been in Pliny's dense forest that you can sometimes come across beside *Aquae*

Citiliae but then, when you're spending all your time looking for it, you can't ever find it again; I had eaten of Borametz, the vegetable lamb of Tartary and, although I had never seen it, I could tell him so much about its delightful flavour that it set his mouth watering. I said, "Its flesh is like that of a crayfish, it has the colour of a ruby or a red peach and a flavour like that of both melons and oranges."

As well as that I told him about all the battles, skirmishes and sieges I'd been involved in, adding some where I'd never been because I could see that was what he wanted to hear. He let himself be amused by all my chatter, like children with fairy tales, until they sent him to sleep and I was taken to a well-furnished room where I also straightaway fell asleep in a soft bed, something that had not happened to me for a long time.

I woke much earlier than the rest of the household but, since there was no one to ask where to go, I couldn't leave my room to relieve myself of a load that was not too great but very awkward to hold in for much longer. Then, however, I found a place for that very purpose behind a screen and much better appointed that I could have hoped for in my hour of need. So I quickly sat down to do my business and wondered how far my noble wilderness was preferable to this well-appointed chamber, for there anyone, native or stranger, could squat down straightaway, without having to endure the fear and distress I had just been through. After I had gone over this question and was thinking about Soon-Another's teaching and tricks, I tore a sheet of paper from an exercise book hanging up beside me, in order to use it for that function to which it and its comrades were condemned and kept imprisoned there.

"O," the sheet of paper said, "must I now, in return for my faithful service and after all the years of torment, danger, fear, travail, misery and sorrow I have been through, feel and accept the thanks of the faithless world? O why did not a finch or a robin eat me when I was little and straightaway turn me into dung, so that I would have been able to serve my mother earth immediately and through my inborn fatness help her to produce a lovely little forest flower or herb, instead of having to wipe a vagrant's bottom and come to my final end in the shithouse. Or why am I not being used in the closet of the king of France, whose arse is being wiped by Henry of Navarre? I would derive much greater honour from that than from serving a runaway monk."

"I can tell from the way you talk," I replied, "that you are a worthless fellow and deserve no other grave than the one to which I am about to commit you. It makes no difference whether it is a king or a beggar who buries you in such a stinking place, of which you speak in such a coarse and impolite manner but which I was delighted to find. If, however, you have some point to make regarding your innocence and the services you have rendered to the human race, then do so; since everyone in the house is still asleep, I will be happy to grant you an audience and perhaps, depending on what I hear, preserve you from your impending doom.

To this he answered, razor-sharp, "Initially my ancestors, according to Pliny, Book 20, chapter 23, were found on their own ground in a wood where they lived in freedom and spread their kind. Then, as uncultivated plants, they were forced into the service of mankind and given the name of hemp. It was from them that I sprang as a seed in the days of King

Wenceslas in the village of Goldscheuer, which is said to be the place where the best hemp seed in the world comes from. There the man who had grown me took me off my parents' stalk in early spring and sold me to a merchant, who mixed me with other hemp seeds and took us to market where he sold me to a local farmer; from each peck he earned half a gold guilder because we had suddenly risen in price and become expensive. So that merchant was the second to make a profit from me after the one who had grown me and first sold me.

"The farmer who had bought me cast me into a well-tended fertile field where I had to rot and die off in the stench of dung from horses, pigs, cows and other beasts. But I put forth a tall, proud hemp stalk, into which I was gradually transformed, and in my innocence immediately said to myself, "Now you will become a fruitful multiplier of your race and bring forth more seeds than any has ever done before. But hardly had I preened myself with this imagined future, than I had to hear lots of passers-by say, 'Look what a big field full of gallows-weed,' which I and my brothers took as an ill omen for us. But then we were comforted by some honest old farmers, who said, 'See what excellent fine hemp that is!'

"Unfortunately we soon realised that the humans, because of their greed and indigence, were not going to leave us there to propagate our kind, for while we were thinking we were about to bring forth seeds, various strong lads came and tore us mercilessly out of the ground and tied us up in sheaves, like captured miscreants. For this they received their wages, that is the third profit men made out of us.

"But that was far from the end, in fact our sufferings and the tyranny of humanity was only just beginning as they sought to transform us, a renowned plant! into pure poetry (as some call the beer they like so much). We were carried into a deep pit, packed in one on top of the other and weighed down with stones, as if we were being crushed in a press; and from that came the fourth profit, made by those who carried out this process. Then the pits were filled with water, so that we were swamped in it, as if they were trying to drown us, regardless of the fact that our strength was already weakened. We were left in this press until the leaves that adorned us but were already withered, had rotted away and we ourselves almost suffocated and died. Then they ran off the water, took us out and laid us on a green meadow where we were treated now by the sun, then the rain, then the wind so that the air itself, horrified at our wretched situation, changed and made everything around us stink, so that no one at all walked past without holding their nose or at least saying, "Yeuch!" But despite that, those who had treated us like this pocketed the fifth profit.

We had to remain in this state until the wind and sun together had robbed us of our last drop of moisture and, together with the rain, bleached us, at which our farmer sold us to a hemp processor for the sixth profit. Thus we had our fourth master since I had been a tiny hempseed. He put us in a shed, for a brief rest, until he had enough time and labourers to subject us to more torture. Then when the autumn came and all the other work in the fields was over, he took us out one after the other and put us in a little room, two dozen at a time, behind the stove, which he made very hot, as if we had to sweat out the French disease. In that infernal heat I often thought we were in danger of going up in flames, together with the house, which does in fact often happen.

"Once this had made us more flammable than the best lucifer, he gave us over to an even more severe torturer who strewed us under the crusher a handful at a time until all our internal parts were a hundred thousand times smaller than happens to the worst of murderers on the wheel, hitting us afterwards with a flail so that our broken parts should fall out cleanly. It looked as if he had gone mad as the sweat – as well as something that begins and ends with the same letter – came pouring out of him. Thus he became the seventh human to make a profit out of us.

"We thought that now nothing more could be devised to continue our torture. This was mainly because we had been so separated from each other, but then put together and mingled, that none of us knew who or what we were and every bit of flax or bast had to admit we were broken hemp. But then we were put on a board and rubbed and grated as if they wanted to make us into asbestos, cotton wool, silk or at least the most delicate flax of all; and the man who did all this made the eighth profit men had gained from me and my kin.

"That very same day I was handed over, as a well-rubbed and flayed piece of hemp, to a few old women and young apprentice girls, who subjected me to the worst torture I had suffered so far: they took me apart on their hackles in such a way that it is beyond belief: first they heckled out of me the oakum, then the hemp for spinning and finally the poor-quality hemp, until eventually I was praised as delicate hemp and excellent merchandise. To prepare me for sale I was combed out, packed and placed in a damp cellar so that I should be even more delicate to the touch and heavier in weight. In this state I was once more granted a brief rest, happy that having survived so much sorrow and suffering I had become a material that was necessary and useful to you humans. Now the aforementioned women had received the ninth profit from me, which I found strangely comforting and it gave me hope (because we had reached nine, a most wonderful, angelic number) that our ordeal was now over."

Chapter 12

"The next market day my owner took me to a room where I was examined, recognised as genuine merchandise, weighed and sold on to a middleman, loaded onto a cart, taken to Strasbourg, delivered to the warehouse, examined once more, adjudged good and sold to a merchant, who had me taken to his house in a handcart and stored in a clean room. In the course of these transactions, my former master, the hemp-preparer, received the tenth, the examiner the eleventh, the weigher the twelfth, the customs official the thirteenth, the middleman the fourteenth, the carrier the fifteenth, the warehouse the sixteenth and the men who took me to the merchant's house in the handcart the seventeenth profit. These latter also pocketed the eighteenth profit, since they took me in their cart to the boat on which I was taken down the Rhine to Zwolle. I cannot say how many people received customs duty or some other payment, and thus profited from me, because I was packed so tightly I couldn't see or hear anything.

"In Zwolle I once more had a brief rest before I was separated from the medium or English wares, once more closely examined and tortured, pulled apart, beaten and hackled until I was so pure and delicate that I could have been spun into the finest yarn. After that I was taken to Amsterdam, bought and sold, then handed over to the female sex, who made me into delicate thread; during their work they kept kissing and licking me, so that I thought all my suffering must have reached its end. Shortly after that, however, I was washed, wound, handed over to the weaver, smeared with weaver's paste, stretched out on the loom and made into fine Dutch linen, then bleached and sold to a Dutch merchant, who then sold me by the yard.

"Until I got that far, however, I was much reduced; the first and coarsest oakum that was taken from me was spun into wicks, boiled in cow dung and then burnt. The old women span another part that was taken from me into coarse yarn, which was woven into ticking and sackcloth, while a third part made fairly coarse yarn which, despite that, was still sold as hemp; the fourth part was made into yarn that was spun and woven into cloth, but was no comparison with me, never mind with the strong ropes that were made from my comrades, the other hemp stalks that had been scutched. That I and my kind are of great use to the human race and how much profit various people derive from it is almost more than I can tell. The last part that was taken I suffered myself when the weaver threw a couple of balls of thread from me at the thieving mice.

"A noblewoman acquired me from the above-mentioned merchant and cut the cloth into pieces, which she gave her servants as New Year presents. The piece I mostly went into was given to the lady's maid, who made a chemise out of it in which she looked very attractive with me. Here I learnt that not all those who are called maids are maids, for not only the steward but also the master himself lay with her, for she wasn't ugly. But that didn't last for long, for eventually the mistress herself saw how her maid was taking her place. However, she didn't rant and rage, but behaved like a sensible woman, paid off her maid and gave her a friendly farewell. The master, however, was not best pleased when he saw such a tasty piece taken from him and asked his wife why she was getting rid of the maid, who was so nimble, deft and hardworking. She, however, replied, 'Don't worry, my Lord, from now on I will do her work myself.'

"After this my maid set off with her luggage, which included her best chemise, for her home in Cambrai. She was also carrying a fairly heavy purse, for she had earned quite a lot from her master and mistress and had saved up quite a lot. Once there she didn't find such a lucrative position as the one she had had to leave, but she did find several admirers who became infatuated with her and brought her clothes to wash and to mend, for that was what she had made her profession, intending to make a living by it. Among them was a young braggart whom she hoodwinked into thinking she was a maid. The wedding was held, but after a honeymoon month it became clear that the savings and income of the young couple were not sufficient to keep them in the way they had been accustomed to with their masters. And since there was a shortage of soldiers in the land of Luxembourg, my young woman's husband became a cornet, perhaps because another had taken his place and had given him a pair of horns.

"By that time I was becoming fairly thin and worn, so the woman cut me up into nappies, for she was expecting a child. Afterwards, when she had given birth, I was daily dirtied by the said bastard and just as often washed clean again. Eventually this made us so weak we were no use any longer and were thrown out by the woman. However, we were picked up by her landlady (who was a good housekeeper), washed and put with other similar rags in the attic. We had to stay there until a fellow came from Épinal, who collected such rags from all over the place. He took us back with him to a paper mill where he handed us over to some old women, who immediately tore us into strips and we wailed to each other in our misery.

"That, however, wasn't the end of it. In the paper mill we were pounded into pulp, so that no one could tell that we were hemp or flax, and eventually even pickled in lime and alum and then washed out in water, so that you could truly say of us that we had completely disappeared. But all of a sudden I found that I had been made into a fine sheet of writing paper and then, through further processes, turned with other comrades into a quire and then into a ream. We were put through the press again and sent to Zurzach for the forthcoming trade fair, where we were sold to a merchant from Zürich. He took us home and then sold the ream of which I was part to the steward of a great lord, who made us into an account book. But before all this could happen, I must have gone through the hands of thirty-six people since I'd been a rag.

"The steward loved this book, of which as an honest sheet I made up two pages, as much as Alexander the Great did Homer; it was his Virgil that Augustus used to study so diligently; his Oppian which Anthony, the son of Emperor Severus, read so assiduously; his Pliny the Younger that Largius Licinius valued so highly; his Tertullian that Cyprian would take up so often; his *Paedia Cyri*, that Scipio made so popular; his *Philolaus Pythagoricus* in which Plato took such pleasure; his Speusippus, that Aristotle loved so much;

his Cornelius Tacitus in which Emperor Tacitus delighted so much; his Comminaeus, whom Charles the Fifth respected above all writers – all in all it was his Bible that he studied day and night. But that was not to ensure that the calculations were honest and correct, but in order to cover his thefts, his embezzlement and other knavery and enter everything in such a way that the account book was flawless.

"Once this book was full, it was put aside until the lord and his wife went the way of all flesh, and during that time I enjoyed a good rest. However, once the heirs had shared out the estate, they tore up the book and used it for all kinds of packing paper, on which occasion I was put round a fur-trimmed coat so that neither the cloth nor the trimming should be spoilt. And that was how I was brought here and, after being unpacked, condemned to this place where, as a reward for my services to the human race, I was to come to my end, from which, however, you could save me."

I replied, "Since your growth and reproduction depends on the richness of the soil, which is maintained by animal excrement, and since you are, anyway, in the habit of talking in a coarse manner about such things, then it is right and proper that you should return to your place of origin, to which your own master has condemned you."

With that, I carried out the sentence, but the sharp-tongued rascal said, "Just as you are treating me now, so will Death deal with you when he turns you back into the earth from which you came, and nothing will be able to put that off, though you could have saved me from that fate this time."

74

Chapter 13

The previous evening I had lost a list of all the tricks I had previously used and written down so that I would not forget them; not contained in the list were the manner and means by which they could be carried out. As an example I will set down the beginning of such a list here:

"To make a fuse so that it has no smell, which often gives musketeers away so that their attacks come to nothing.

To make a fuse that still burns even when it is wet.

To prepare gunpowder so that it doesn't burn even if you put red-hot steel in it; this is very useful for fortresses that have to store lots of this dangerous stuff.

To shoot men or birds with powder alone so that they stay lying down as if dead for a while, before getting up again unharmed.

To give a person double strength without using Carline thistle and other forbidden things.

To arrange quickly for the enemy's guns to shatter, if you are prevented from spiking them during an attack.

To spoil someone's musket so that it makes all the game run back into the woods, until it has been cleaned out with a special substance.

To hit the black in the target more often when you put your musket on your shoulder and turn your back to the target, than when you aim in the normal way.

A trick to ensure that you are not hit by a bullet.

To make an instrument by which during a quiet night you can, miraculously, hear everything that sounds or is said at an incredible distance (which is otherwise beyond the human ear and impossible); very useful for sentinels, especially during sieges," etc.

Thus many such tricks were described in the list, which my host had found and picked up. He came to me in my little room, showed me the list and asked whether it was possible for these to be carried out by natural means. He found that difficult to believe, but he had to admit that in his youth, when he was a boy with Field Marshal von Schauenburg in Italy, several men claimed that the Princes of Savoy were all secure against bullets. The Field Marshal had the idea of testing this out on Prince Thomas, whom he had besieged in a castle. The two sides had agreed on an hour's truce, to bury the dead and have negotiations, and he called over a Corporal who could trim a burning candle with his musket at fifty paces without putting it out. He ordered this man to watch the Prince, who had come to the battlements for the conference and, the moment the agreed time for the truce had passed, to fire a bullet at him. This Corporal kept his eye on the time and on the Prince during the truce. And when the first stroke of the bell sounded for the end of the truce and both of them were withdrawing into safety, he squeezed the trigger. But his musket unexpectedly failed and the Prince was behind the battlements before he could cock his musket again. At this the Corporal pointed out a Swiss member of the Prince's bodyguard to the Field Marshal, took aim and hit him so that he went tumbling down, which clearly showed that there was something in the story that no prince of Savoy could be killed or wounded by a musket shot. It was, though, impossible to tell whether that was the result of this kind of trick or because the princely house enjoyed a special dispensation from God since it came from the race of the royal prophet David.

I replied, "I don't know that either, but what I do know is that the listed tricks are natural and not magic." And, I went on, if he refused to believe that, he should tell me which one he thought was the most amazing and impossible, and I would try that one out for him, provided it was not one that required a long time and a particular opportunity to carry it out, since I had to leave immediately and continue on my journey. To that he replied that to him what seemed the most impossible was that gunpowder would not burn when fire was applied to it, unless I poured the powder into water first. If I could show that done by natural means, then he would believe all the other tricks without seeing them, even though there were more than sixty of them. I told him to bring me enough gunpowder for one shot and another substance that I needed, together with a flame and he would immediately see that the trick worked. Once he had done that, I got him to proceed in the right sequence, then to light the powder. But he could do no more than gradually burn a few grains even though he spent fifteen minutes trying; all that happened was that however hard he tried all he managed to do was to extinguish both the fuse and the charcoal in the powder as well as the red-hot iron.

"Yes," he said at last, "but now the powder is spoilt."

However I replied by deed rather than word and without more ado made the powder flare up before you could count to sixteen, even though he hardly touched it with the flame.

"O," he said, "if they had known that in Zürich, they would not have suffered such great damage recently when their gunpowder magazine was struck by lightning."

Since he was now convinced that this trick was not done by supernatural means, he immediately wanted to know how a man could protect himself against musket shots, but to tell him that didn't suit me. He tried to persuade me with flattery and promises but I told him I needed neither money nor wealth so then he turned to threats but I replied that they were obliged to allow pilgrims to continue on their way to Einsiedeln. He then accused me of ingratitude for the hospitality I'd received; in answer to that I pointed out he had already learnt enough for that. Since, however, he kept going on at me, I decided to deceive him, for anyone who wanted to learn this trick from me through affection or force would have to be a highly placed person. And since I realised that he didn't care whether it was done with words or crosses, I deceived him in the way Soon-Another had deceived me so that I didn't have to lie but he still didn't know how the trick really worked. To do this I gave him this note:

"The following words will protect you from being hit by a bullet: *Asa, vitom, raharhi, eni, mendiem rezinah, orinkim, nas aheplom, nahlres, inabe elcit, bex, arwes, oghum, ven Barbo nei, alonade, sos, ani, wient, alche, elame, arnam, asa, clevo, nei, viyet, aroli, druan, Velsalash, Hernoda, edi, szyew, phrosky, qwuky, mewes, eltiria, ele, harlari erbsa, nei, leasimi, nai elerfrisa Vrakeszox.*"

When I handed him the note, he believed it because it was gobbledygook no one could understand, as he thought. But, still, it helped me to get away from him and he even went so far as to offer me a few talers to help me on my way; these I refused, but I was more than happy to accept breakfast before I left. So I walked down the Rhine towards Eglisau but on the way I stopped and sat for a while at the place where the river has its waterfall and, with a great roar, part of the water turns into liquid dust.

As I walked along I began to wonder if I hadn't done too much by hoodwinking my host, who had given me such a friendly reception. At some time in the future he might, perhaps, show the note as something absolutely certain to his children or friends, and they might then trust it and, putting themselves unnecessarily in danger, come to an untimely end. Who else would then be responsible for their death than me?

So I thought I should turn back and confess what I had done. But I was concerned that, if he got me in his claws again, he would deal more harshly with me than before or at least get his own back on me, so I continued on to Eglisau. There I managed to beg food, drink, a bed for the night and a half sheet of paper. On the latter I wrote, "Noble, pious and esteemed Sir, I would like to thank you again for the comfortable lodging and pray that the Lord will reward you for it a thousand times over; otherwise I am concerned that you might in future put yourself too much in danger and tempt God because you learnt from me the excellent trick to ward off bullets. Therefore I want to warn you, Sir, and explain the trick so that it will not bring you misfortune and harm."

I wrote: "The following words will protect you from being hit by a bullet. To understand it correctly, however, you must take the middle letters out of all the non-German words, which are neither magic nor have any power, and write them down in order, and you will read, 'Stand in a place where no one can see you and you will be safe.'

Follow that advice, Sir, keep me in your thoughts and do not accuse me of deception in commending us both to the care of God, who alone protects those to whom he is inclined. Dated etc, etc."

The next day they refused to let me through because I had no money to pay the toll, so I had to sit there for a good two hours before an honest man came who paid it for me out of charity. The man must have been an executioner, for the customs officer said to him, "What do you think, Master Christian, will you be bringing this pilgrim's journey to an early end?"

"I don't know," Master Christian replied, "I've never practised my skills on pilgrims the way I have on you customs officers."

The customs officer looked rather put out at that, but I just continued on my way to Zürich, where I arranged for my letter to be sent back to Schaffhausen, because I was still worried about the business with the supposed protection against bullets.

Chapter 14

During that time I learnt how difficult it is to travel round the world with no money, even if you're happy not to have any to keep body and soul together. Other pilgrims, who did have money and were going to Einsiedeln, were sitting on the boat sailing up the lake. I, on the other hand, had to go the long way round on foot because I couldn't pay the fare. However, I didn't worry about this, I just did shortish distances each day and made do with any shelter I happened to find, and would even have spent the night in a charnel house if I'd had to. And if someone insisted on taking me in because of my odd appearance, hoping to hear strange tales from me, I gave them what they wanted, I told them all sorts of trumped-up stories of things I pretended to have seen, heard or experienced on my long travels; I even had no compunction about relating the ideas, lies and fancies of the old writers and poets, presenting them as true, as if I had been there myself: for example that I had seen a race of people from the Pontus, called Thibians, who had two eyeballs in one eye and the likeness of a horse in the other, proving it by quoting Philarchus; that I had been at the source of the Ganges with the Astomi, who neither eat nor have mouths but who, according to Pliny, nourish themselves solely from the smells they take in through their noses. I also claimed to have been with the Bithynian women in Scythia and the Triballi in Illyria, who have two eyeballs in each eye, as reported by Apollonides and Hesigonus; a few years previously, I claimed, I had got on well with the people who lived on Mili Mountain and who, as Megasthenes says, have feet like foxes with eight toes on each foot; I also said that for a while I had lived with the Troglodites in the west who, as Ctesias testifies, have neither heads nor necks, but their eyes, noses and mouths on their chests, and also with the Monosceles or Sciopodes, who have only one foot, with which they shelter their whole bodies from rain and sunshine, but with that single large foot they can outrun a deer. I said I had also seen the Anthropophagi in Scythia and the Kaffers in Africa who eat human flesh; the Andabatea who fight and knock each other down, with their eyes closed, the Agriophani, who eat the flesh of lions and panthers; the Arimphei who sleep safely under the trees without shelter; the Bactriani, who live in such moderation that no vice is more hated than guzzling and boozing; the Samoyeds who live beneath the snow beyond the Moskva; the island dwellers in the straits of Hormuz in the Persian Gulf, where it is so hot they sleep in the water; the Greenlanders, whose women wear trousers; the Berbers who execute all those over fifty, sacrificing them to their gods; the Indians on the Pacific Ocean beyond the Straits of Magellan whose women have short hair, the men themselves, however, long ponytails; the Condei who live on snakes; the Baltic peoples beyond Livonia who turn into werewolves at certain times of the year; the Gapii who execute their old people by starving them to death once they have reached seventy; the black Tartars whose children are born with their teeth; the Getae, who hold everything in common, even their women; the Himantopodes who crawl along the ground like snakes; Brazilians that receive strangers with tears and the Mosineci who do so with blows. Yes, I had even seen the Moon Women who, as Herodotus maintains, lay eggs and hatch people out of them who grow to be ten times bigger than in Europe.

I had also seen many miraculous wells, for example the one that is the source of the Vistula, the water of which turns to stone with which people build houses; similarly the well at Zepusio in Hungary, the water of which eats away iron or, to be more precise, turns it into a substance which is subsequently made into copper by smelting since the rain turns into vitriol; at the same place there is also a poisonous well and if the ground is watered with it, nothing but snakeweed will grow, that waxes and wanes with the moon; there is another well there that is warm in the winter but is frozen solid in the summer and the ice can be used to cool the wine; I had also seen the two wells in Ireland, one of which, if you drink it, makes you old and grey, the other young and pretty, the well at Ängstlen in Switzerland that only runs when the stock comes from the meadow to drink; then there are various wells in Iceland where the one has hot, the other cold water, the third produces sulphur, the fourth molten wax; and the waterholes in St. Stephan in the Saanen area of Switzerland, which people use to foretell the weather, for it becomes cloudy when it's about to rain and is clear when fine weather is in store; then there is the Schantli stream at Obernähenheim in Alsace that never flows unless some great disaster such as famine, death or war is to visit the country; the poisonous wells in Arcadia that caused the death of Alexander the Great; the waters of Sybaris that turn grey hair black; the Acquae Suessanae, that make barren women fruitful; the waters of the Island of Ischia that take away gravel and stone; those at Clitumno that turn oxen white if they are bathed in it; those at Solennio that heal the wounds of love; the Aleos Well that lights the fires of love; the well in Persia out of which pure oil springs and the one not far from Kronweissenburg with grease for cartwheels; the water on the Isle of Naxos on which you can get drunk; the Fountain of Arethusa that has nothing but sugar water.

I was also able to describe all the famous marshes, lakes, ponds and swamps, for example the lake at Zircknitz in Carinthia, which, when it dries out, leaves fish five feet long which the peasants catch; they then sow seed in the bottom of the lake, mow and harvest the hay, and then in the autumn the lake fills up again with water forty feet deep, which produces the same amount of fish the next spring. The Dead Sea in Judaea, Lake Leomondo on Lemnos that is twenty-five miles long and has many islands, including one floating island which together with the cattle and everything on it is driven to and fro by the wind. I could talk about many lakes: the Federsee in Swabia, Lake Constance, Lake Pilatus on Fräkmuntegg mountain, Kamarina in Sicily, Lacu Bebeide in Thessaly, Gigeo in Lydia, Marette in Egypt, Stymphalus in Arcadia, Lasconio in Bythinia, Icomede in Ethiopia, Thesprotio in Ambratia, Trasimene in Umbria, the Sea of Azov and many more.

I said I had also seen all the famous rivers in the world, for example the Rhine and the Danube in Germany, the Elbe in Saxony, the Moldau in Bohemia, the Inn in Bavaria, The

Volga in Russia, the Thames in England, the Tajo in Spain, the Amphrisum in Thessaly, the Nile in Egypt, the Jordan in Judaea, the Bug in Scythia, the Bagradas near Carthage, the Ganges in India, the Rio de la Plata in America, the Euphrates in Mesopotamia, the Tiber in Italy, the Cidnum in Cilicia, the Acheloun between Aetolia and Acarnania, the Dnieper in Thrace and the Sabbaticus in Syria, that only flows for six days, disappearing on the seventh; then a river in Sicily in which, according to Aristotle, birds that have been strangled or suffocated are brought back to life; then also the Gallum in Phyrgia which, Ovid claims, makes you mad if you drink of it; I had also seen the Plinys' well in Dordona and tried it myself to see that it does indeed put out candles but relight those that have gone out when you dip them into it; I was also at the well in Apollonia, called the Cup of the Nymphs, which, as Theopompus says, tells anyone who drinks of it all the misfortune they are going to meet.

I could also boast about other wonders of the world, such as the Calaminic Woods, that can be driven from one place to another, wherever you want them to be; I had also been in the Cimminic Forest where I hadn't to stick my pilgrim's staff in the ground, for everything that goes into the earth there immediately takes root, so that you can never pull it out again, for it quickly grows into a tall tree; I had also seen the two woods, that Pliny mentions, which are now triangular, now quadrangular, now round; not to mention the rock that you can sometimes move with one finger, sometimes not at all, however hard you try.

To sum up, when I said I not only knew about strange and marvellous things but had seen everything with my own eyes, even if it was famous things like the seven wonders of the world, the Tower of Babel and such buildings that had disappeared hundreds of years ago, and did the same when I talked about birds, animals, fish and plants, it was not just for the pleasure of telling lies but to please my hosts, who desired to hear that kind of thing – however, when I met intelligent people, I didn't go to such extremes. Thus I managed to get to Einsiedeln, made my devotions there and then headed for Bern, not just in order to see that city, but to go from there through Savoy to Italy.

Chapter 15

My journey went pretty well for I found kind-hearted people who were happy to give me both lodging and food from their plenty; and they were all the happier to do that because they saw that I neither asked for nor accepted money, even when I was offered a few coppers. In the town I saw a well-dressed man, who was still very young, with children running round who called him father. I was surprised at this, for I didn't know that such sons married young so that they could become officials and find posts in the prefectures all the sooner. This man saw me begging at the doors of several houses and when I made a low bow as I passed by him (for I couldn't doff my hat to him since I went bare-headed), instead of running up to him in the street as some shameless beggars do, he put his hand in his pocket and said, "Hey, why aren't you asking for alms? Look, there's a copper for you." I replied, "I could well imagine, sir, that you don't carry a loaf of bread around with you, so that is why I didn't ask you; I don't seek money for that is not right for beggars."

By that time there was, as usual, a crowd gathered round and he went on, "You must be a proud beggar if you spurn money."

"No, sir. I would not have you believe that I scorn money so that it will not make me proud."

He asked, "Then where are you going to spend the night if you have no money?"

"If God and good folk were kind enough to allow me to take my rest, which I sorely need, in that shed, I would have what I need and rest content."

He then said, "If I could be sure that you had no lice, I could take you in and give you a proper bed."

For my part I replied that I had as few lice as I had coins, but I wasn't sure whether it would be advisable for me to sleep in a bed, because that might spoil me and make me abandon my habit of living a hard life.

At this point a fine gentleman came along to whom the young man said, "Look there, another Diogenes the Cynic, as God's my witness."

"O come now, cousin," the old man said, "what are you saying? Has he barked at someone and bitten them? Give him alms and let him go on his way."

The young man replied, "He doesn't want money, cousin, nor any other kindness people want to do him." Then he told the old man everything I had said and done.

"Ah!" said the old man, "Now that makes sense." And he told his servants to take me to an inn and to promise to pay the landlord for everything I might consume that night. As I went off the young man shouted after me that I was to be sure to come and see him in the morning and he would give me a good cold collation to take on my way.

So I escaped from my situation in which I was hounded worse than I can describe, but I just came out of the frying pan into the fire, for the inn was full of wild drunks who gave me more trouble than I'd had on my journey so far. They all wanted to know who I was: one said I must be a spy, another that I was an Anabaptist, the third that I was a fool, the fourth thought I was a saintly prophet but most that I was the Wandering Jew, as I have already mentioned above – they almost got me to show them that I hadn't been circumcised. Finally the landlord took pity on me and dragged me away from them saying, "Leave the man alone. I don't know who's the bigger fool, him or you." And then he had me led away to sleep.

The next day I went to the young man's house to get the breakfast he had promised. The man himself wasn't at home but his wife came down with the children, perhaps to see the strange person I was that her husband must have told her about. I learnt from what she said, as if she thought I ought to have known, that her husband was a member of the Senate and was in certain hope of getting appointed to a senior position that very day. I should just wait a while, she said, he would soon be home. As we were talking, he came down the street, to my mind looking nothing like so cheerful as he had been the previous day.

As soon as he reached the door, she said to him, "Well, darling, what are you now?" But he ran straight up the steps, saying as he passed her, "A turd, that's what I am now."

At this I thought, 'Now all the goodwill is going to turn sour,' so I slipped quietly away from the door. However, the children followed me to see their fill of my strange person and others joined them, to whom they boasted what an honourable position their father had obtained. "Yes," they said to all those who came along, "our father has become a turd," and I had to laugh at their simplicity and foolishness.

Since I now realised that I did far less well in the towns than in the country, I decided not to go into any more towns, if it was at all possible to avoid them. So out in the country I made do with milk, cheese, butter and the occasional piece of bread that countrymen gave me until I had almost crossed the border into Savoy. Once in that region I was walking towards the seat of some nobleman through mud that came over my ankles while the rain was bucketing down. When I got close to the aforementioned house it was my good fortune the noble lord himself saw me. He was surprised not only at my dress but at my patience, and since I didn't even want to shelter for a while in such heavy rain, though I had the opportunity to do so, he thought I must be a fool pure and simple. But he did send one of his servants down to me, whether out of pity or curiosity I couldn't say, who said his master wished to know who I was and why I was avoiding his house in such terrible rain.

I replied, "My friend, tell your master I am a ball of variable fortune, an example of change, a mirror of the transience of humanity. However, the reason why I am walking in such a storm is simply that no one has offered me shelter since the rain began."

When the servant told his master this, he said, "Those are not the words of a fool; and anyway, night is falling and no one should throw even a dog out in such miserable weather," and so had me brought into the castle, where I washed my feet and dried out my coat in the servants' quarters.

The knight had a man who was his steward, his children's tutor and, at the same time, his scribe, or secretary as they like

90

to be called now, and this fellow questioned me, asking where had I come from, where was I going, what was my country, my rank? I told him everything about myself, where I came from and where I had lived as a hermit, and that now it was my intention to visit the holy places here and there.

He reported all this to his master, who therefore had me join him at his table for dinner, where I was well fed and, at the lord's request, had to repeat everything about myself and my doings that I had previously told his scribe. He questioned me very precisely about all the details as if he himself were at home there. And when I was taken to bed, he himself came with the servant, who lit the way, and took me into a room that was so well furnished a Count would have been happy with it. I was surprised at this excessive courtesy and could only imagine he was behaving towards me in this way out of pure reverence because I thought I had the appearance of a blessed pilgrim.

But there was something else behind it, for when he was standing in the doorway with his servant and the light, and I was already in bed, he said, "Well, good night, Herr Simplicius, I hope you sleep well. I know that you are not afraid of ghosts, but I can assure you that those that walk in this room can't be driven off with a bullwhip." And with that he locked the door and left me lying there in fear and trembling.

I thought and thought, but for a long time I couldn't remember where this gentleman could have met me, for he specifically called me by my former name. But after brooding over it for a long time I remembered that in Sauerbrunn once, after my friend Heartbrother had died, I had talked about the spirits of the night with some gentlemen and students. Among

91

them were two Swiss brothers who told us marvellous things about their home, where there were strange noises not only during the night, but often by day. I had matched them and rather arrogantly maintained that anyone who was afraid of such ghosts was nothing but a scaredy-cat. At that one of them dressed up in white, sneaked into my room that night and started rattling and rumbling, thinking to frighten me, and then, when I was horrified and lay there rigid with fear, to whip the blanket off me and taunt me and punish me for my arrogance. However, when he started his act, to make me wake up, I slipped out of bed, took up a bullwhip, grabbed the ghost by its wing and said, "When the ghosts are white then maids become women, as they say," and boldly struck out at him until he eventually pulled away from me and found the door.

Now that I remembered this story and thought about what my host had said, it wasn't difficult for me to see what I was in for. I said to myself, "If they were telling the truth about the terrible ghosts in their father's house, then you are doubtless lying in bed in the very room where they make the worst racket. However, if they were just boasting out of boredom, then they will doubtless give you a whipping that will surely take you quite a while to recover from." Pondering these thoughts, I got up with the idea of jumping out of the window, but there were such strong bars everywhere that it was impossible and, what was worst of all, I had no gun, indeed, I didn't even have my strong pilgrim's staff with me, which I could if necessary have used to defend myself. Therefore I lay down in bed again, even though I couldn't sleep, waiting in fear and trembling to see what this terrible night would bring.

When midnight struck, the door opened, even though I had

bolted it on the inside. The first to come in was a dignified, grave person with a long white beard, dressed in the old-fashioned manner in a long gown of white satin with golden flowers and lined with civet fur. He was followed by three further men, also dignified. As they entered, the whole room became as bright as if they had brought torches with them, even though I couldn't actually see a candle or anything like that. I stuck my nose under the blanket, keeping just my eyes out, like a frightened little mouse sitting in its hole to see whether it's safe to go out or not. They, on the other hand, came right up to my bed and had a good look at me, as I did at them. After this had gone on for a while, they all went into one corner of the room, lifted up a stone slab that was there and took out all the things a barber would have if he was going to trim someone's beard. With these they came back to me, placed a chair in the middle of the room and, beckoning and pointing, indicated that I was to get out of bed, sit on the chair and let myself be given a haircut.

When I remained lying down, the leader himself grabbed the blanket in order to pull it off and to force me to sit on the chair. You can imagine the chill that ran down my spine. I held on tight to the blanket and said, "What is it, gentlemen, why do you want to shear me? I'm a poor pilgrim and have nothing other than my own hair to protect my head from wind, rain and sunshine. Moreover you don't look like shearers at all so please leave me unshorn."

To that their leader replied, "We are arch-shearers, we can fleece anyone, but you can help us, you have to promise to help us if you want to remain unshorn."

"If it is in my power to help you," I said, "then I promise

to do everything possible that is necessary to help you. So tell me what I can do."

At this the old one said, "I am the great-grandfather of the present lord of this castle. I started a quarrel with my cousin over two villages that were his lawful property and, by fraudulent cunning, arranged that these three here were appointed to judge the matter. Then, through promises and threats, I got them to award both of those villages to me. Once that had been done, I started to fleece the villagers who were now my subjects, to bleed them dry until I had put together a tidy sum of money. That is now in that corner, where it lies as shearing equipment in order to remind me of the way I fleeced my cousin and the villagers. This money must be returned to the people – for after my death the two villages were returned to their rightful owner – and you will have helped me as much as you can if you tell all this to my great-grandson. To help him to believe you, get him in the morning to take you to the so-called Green Room, where you will find my portrait. Stand in front of that and tell him what you have heard from me."

Once he had finished, he held out his hand and asked me to shake hands as a token of my agreement to do what he asked. However, since I had often heard it said that you shouldn't let a ghost take your hand, I held out the tip of the sheet that burnt away as soon as he had grasped it. The ghosts took their shearing equipment back to the hole, replaced the stone slab over it, put the chair back where it had been before and left the room, one after the other. By now I was sweating like a roast on the fire but was yet bold enough to fall asleep despite my fear.

Chapter 16

It had been light for quite some time when the lord came to my bed with his servant again. "Good morning, Herr Simplicius," he said. "How was it last night? You didn't need a bullwhip?"

"No, Monsieur," I replied. "Those that live here don't need that, the way the one who tried to fool me in Sauerbrunnen did."

"But how was it then?" he went on. "Are you still not afraid of ghosts?"

"I won't say ghosts are fun," I replied, "but nor will I say that I'm afraid of them because of that. How it was you can see in part from this burnt sheet and I will tell you the rest, Sir, once you take me to the Green Room where I will show you the portrait of the main ghost that walks here."

He looked at me in surprise and could easily imagine that I must have talked to the ghosts because I not only knew about the Green Room, that no one had mentioned to me, but also because of the burnt sheet.

"So now," he went on, "you believe the things I told you in Sauerbrunnen?"

"What need do I have of belief," I said, "when I know something through having experienced it myself?"

"Yes," he said, "I'd be willing to pay a thousand guilders to rid the house of this affliction."

To that I said, "You will just have to content yourself with getting rid of it without having to pay one penny; in fact you will actually receive some money."

With that I got out of bed and we both went straight to the Green Room, that was both a drawing room and housed an art collection. On the way there we were joined by my host's brother, the one I had given a whipping in Sauerbrunnen, whom his brother had urgently summoned from his castle some two hours away. Since he had a scowl on his face, I was afraid he might be out for revenge. But I showed no fear at all and when we came to the room I saw, among other fine pictures and antiques, the portrait I was looking for.

"That," I said to the two brothers, "is your great-grandfather who wrongfully took two villages from his cousin, though these villages have now been returned to their rightful owner. Your great-grandfather collected a considerable sum of money from those villages which, while he was alive, he kept under a stone slab in the room where I paid for what I did with the bullwhip in Sauerbrunnen. And that is why he and his helpers appear in the house with such terrible manifestations." I went on to tell them that if they wanted him to come to his rest, they had to take out the money and use it in any way they thought they could justify before God. I would be happy to show them where it was then I would continue of my way, in God's name.

Since I had told them the truth about their great-grandfather and the two villages they presumably thought I would not be lying about the hidden treasure, so they immediately accompanied me to the room where I'd slept. There we lifted the slab over the place out of which the ghosts had taken their shears and put them back again. But all we found there was two earthenware pots that looked quite new. One was filled with red sand, the other with white, at which the brothers' hopes of finding treasure there vanished.

I, however, was not disappointed, for it gave me the opportunity to try out what Theophrastus Paracelsus says, in his *Philosophia Occulta*, about the transmutation of hidden treasures. So I took the two pots and their contents to the smithy, that the owner of the castle had in the forecourt, placed them in the fire and heated them up, as you would if you were smelting metal. After I had let them cool down gradually, we found in the one a mass of the finest gold, in the other a lump of 14-carat silver, so we had no idea what kind of coins had been in them.

By the time we had finished this, lunch was served, but I found that neither the food nor the drink agreed with me and I felt so ill that they had to take me back home to bed; whether it was because in the few previous days I had mortified my flesh too much in the rain or because of the fright I'd had from the ghosts the night before, I couldn't say.

I had to stay in bed for twelve days and if I'd been any worse, I would have died. One good bloodletting did wonders for me, together with the care I received. Meanwhile the two brothers had brought in a goldsmith, without telling me, and had the two melted-down lumps of precious metal tested, because they were concerned there might be some kind of trickery involved. However, when the metals were found to be genuine and no ghost was to be seen anywhere in the castle, they didn't know what to do to honour and reward me; they even saw me as a holy man to whom all secret things were plain and who had been specially sent to them by God to put their house in order again. Thus the lord of the castle himself never left my bedside and was happy when he could just talk with me, and that lasted until I was back in good health again.

During those days the lord told me quite openly that, when he was a young boy, some vagabond had come to see his father and promised to question the ghost and thus free the house from the monster. To do that he had had himself locked in the room where I had slept, but during the night the ghosts such as I had seen had fallen on him, dragged him out of bed, placed him on a chair and, because of his intention, had pinched, shorn and tormented him for several hours, so that in the morning he was found lying there half dead. During that night his beard and hair had turned quite grey, although he had gone to bed in the evening as a thirty-year-old man with black hair. The lord confessed that he had put me in that same room for no other reason than to avenge his brother and to make me believe what he had told me some years ago about those ghosts and I had refused to believe. He then asked me to forgive him and vowed to remain my friend and servant for the rest of his days.

Once I had recovered and was ready to continue on my way, he offered me a horse, clothes and money to buy food, and when I refused everything, he didn't want to let me leave, saying I shouldn't make him the most ungrateful man in the world but at least accept some money to help me on my way, if I was determined to continue my pilgrimage in such wretched clothes.

"Who knows," he said, "when your lordship might need it?"

I had to laugh, and said, "My lord, it surprises me to hear you call me 'lord' when you can see that I am determined to remain a poor beggar."

"Well," he said, "then stay with me for the rest of your life and receive your alms daily at my table."

"My lord," I said, "if I were to do that I would be a greater lord than you yourself? But if your lordship would like to do something for me, I would ask you to have my coat lined because winter is coming."

"Well thank God," he said, "that there is something by which I can show my gratitude." He then gave me a sheepskin until my coat had been lined, which was done with woollen cloth, because I would allow no other lining. Once that had been done, he let me leave, giving me some letters, I could deliver to his relatives, more to recommend me to them than that he had any news he needed to report.

Chapter 17

So I set out with the intention of visiting the most sacred and famous places in the world thus poorly clad, for I imagined that God had looked down on me graciously. I assumed He was pleased with my patience and voluntary poverty and would therefore help me along the way, just as I had felt God's helping hand and grace in the castle.

In the first place where I lodged for the night I was joined by a messenger who claimed he was going the same way as me, that is to Loreto. Since I didn't know the way nor speak the language very well, and he claimed he didn't walk particularly fast, we agreed to stay together as company for each other. He also generally had things to do in the places where I had to deliver the letters the lord of the castle had given me, where we were fed in princely fashion. When, however, he had to go to an inn, he insisted I join him and paid for me, which I didn't want to accept for long because I imagined I was helping him to squander his hard-earned wages. But he said he profited from my company, for in the places where I had to deliver letters he could live for free and save his money.

Thus we crossed the high mountains and came to the fruitful plains of Italy, and it was only there that my companion told me he had been instructed by the lord of the castle to accompany me and pay my expenses. He therefore begged me to stay with him and accept the alms the lord had sent me of his own free will, rather than having to extract them from all kinds of unwilling people. I was surprised at the lord's honesty, but I still didn't want the disguised messenger to stay with me any longer or pay any more of my expenses. So I told him I had already had more than enough from him, for which I could never pay him back; in reality, however, I had vowed to reject all human comfort and humbly rely on God in all my wanderings. I would not have accepted his guidance on the way, nor food and drink, if I had known he had been specifically sent to provide me with that.

When he saw that I simply did not want his company any longer and turned away from him, asking him to give his master my greetings and thank him again for all he had done for me, my companion bade me a sad farewell, saying, "Goodbye then, worthy Simplicius. And if at the moment you cannot believe how eager my master is to do you good, you will find that out when the lining of your coat is torn or you have to mend it yourself." And with that he went off as if blown away by the wind.

"What can the fellow have meant by that?" I wondered. "I can't believe his master regrets having given me the lining. No, Simplicius," I said to myself, "he didn't send this messenger all this way at his own cost just to remind me here that he had my coat lined, there must be something else behind it."

So I examined my coat and found that he had had one ducat after another sewn in under the seam, so that I had been carrying a large sum of money without realising it. I was quite disturbed by this and I wished he had kept his money and I kept wondering what I should do with it. At first I thought of taking it back to him, then of using it to set up house or to buy an annuity, but eventually I decided to use it to go and see Jerusalem, a journey that was impossible without money.

After that I went straight to Loreto and from there to Rome. After I had been there for a while and made my devotions, I met a number of pilgrims who also intended to see the Holy Land and accompanied a man from Genoa among them to his home town, where we looked for an opportunity to cross the Mediterranean. We didn't have to ask for long before we found a ship already loaded with merchandise bound for Alexandria and only waiting for a fair wind. What a strange, even godlike thing is money among the worldly! Because of my shabby appearance, the master of the ship would not have taken me on board if I had introduced myself to him with a mere copper instead of a golden handshake, for when he saw and heard me for the first time he flatly refused my request. However, as soon as I showed him a handful of ducats that I was going to use for my journey, the deal was done without further ado, without my even having to sign an agreement about the fare; he immediately told me what food and other necessities I should provide myself with for the journey. I did as he advised and then sailed off with him in God's name.

During the whole crossing there was no danger from either storms or adverse winds, but several times the master had to avoid pirates, who appeared over the horizon and made as if they were going to attack us. He knew that, given his ship's speed, it was better to flee from them than for us to try and defend ourselves. Thus we arrived in Alexandria sooner than the sailors on our ship thought possible, which I considered a good omen. I paid for my journey and went to stay with the French, who tend to be everywhere, and from them I learnt that at the moment it was impossible for me to continue on to Jerusalem because the Pasha of Damascus was at war, having rebelled against his emperor, with the result that no caravans, however strong they were, could go from Egypt into Judaea, for they would be putting themselves in danger of losing everything.

At that time in Alexandria, where the air is unhealthy anyway, a disease had broken out, because of which many people had withdrawn from the city to other places, especially the European merchants, who were more afraid of dying than the Turks and Arabs. I went overland with one such company to Rosetta, a large town on the Nile. From there we took a boat and sailed up the Nile to a place about one hour away from the great city of Cairo. We disembarked at midnight and rested there until it was light, when we continued on to Cairo, where I met people from all sorts of nations. In that city there were as many strange plants as people, but what seemed strangest of all to me was that now and then the inhabitants, in specially made ovens, hatched out hundreds of young chickens, whose eggs the hens had never touched since they had laid them. It was usually old women who saw to this.

I have never seen such a large, densely populated city where it was cheaper to eat than this one. Despite that, the ducats I had left were gradually disappearing and, even though life there wasn't expensive, I could easily work out that I couldn't last until the Pasha of Damascus' rebellion had ended and the route I must take to go to Jerusalem was safe. I therefore gave full rein to my desire to see other things I was curious about; among them was a place across the Nile where mummy powder was dug up and which I visited several times: the pyramids of the pharaoh and of Rhodope. I got to know the way so well that I could guide strangers there by myself. The last time, however, it turned out badly. I was going with some people to the Egyptian graves to find mummia at a place where there are five pyramids, when we were attacked by Arab robbers, who had come to capture the ostrich-hunters; they caught us and took us by hidden ways across the wilderness to the Red Sea, where they sold us one by one.

Chapter 18

I was the only one left, for when four of the leading robbers saw that silly people laughed at my thick Swiss beard and long hair, which were unusual for them, they decided to exploit this. They took me for themselves, separated from the rest of the band, took off my coat and covered my private parts with beautiful moss that grows on some trees in the woods of Arabia Felix, and since I went barefoot and bareheaded anyway, it all made a most strange and unfamiliar sight. They took me like this as a wild man to the towns and villages on the Red Sea and got people to pay to see me, telling them they had found and captured me in *Arabia Deserta*, far from any human habitation. I was not allowed to say a word to the people, and they threatened to kill me if I did. I found this hard, because I could already gabble a bit of Arabic and I was allowed to talk when I was alone with them. I told them I was happy with their business, for they gave me the same food and drink they had themselves, which was mostly rice and mutton. At night and when we were travelling by day they allowed me to cover myself with my coat, in which there were still a few ducats hidden.

In this shape and form I crossed the Red Sea because my

four masters wanted to visit the cities and market towns on both sides. In a short time they collected a large sum of money with me until we finally came to a large trading city, where a Turkish pasha held court. There were people from countries all over the world there because it was the place where Indian merchandise was unloaded and then transported overland to Aleppo and Cairo to be shipped across the Mediterranean. Once there two of my masters, after they had received permission from the authorities, went with shawms to the main places in the town announcing that anyone who wanted to see the wild man, that had been caught in the stony desert of Arabia, should go to this or that place. In the meantime the others took me to our lodgings where they prepared me: they combed my hair and beard most delicately, taking more care over it than I had ever done, so that not the least hair was lost, because they earned so much money from it.

An incredibly large, jostling throng gathered with some men among them who, as I could tell from their dress, were Europeans. Well, I thought, now your release is at hand and the fraud and villainy of your captors will be revealed. But I held my tongue until I heard some of them speaking German and Dutch, others French and Italian. When I heard the one or the other of them say something about me, I could contain myself no longer and managed to put together enough of the Latin I hadn't used for a long time (so that all the Europeans should understand at the same time) to say, "Gentlemen, in Christ's name I beg you all to rescue me from the hands of these robbers who have made a spectacle of me for their knavish ends."

As soon as I had said that, one of my captors whipped out his sabre to stop me speaking, even though he hadn't understood what I'd said. The honest Europeans, however, held him back and I then said in French, "I am a German and I wanted to make a pilgrimage to Jerusalem. I had permits from the pashas of Alexandria and Cairo but could not go on because of the war in Damascus. While I was waiting in Cairo for an opportunity to continue my journey, these fellows captured me and other honest people just outside the city and carried us off. They have tricked thousands into giving them money by making a show of me."

Then I begged the Germans, as my countrymen, not to leave me there. My captors still refused to give me up, but among the throng there were people from the authorities in Cairo, who testified that they had seen me six months ago in that city wearing clothes. At that the Europeans appealed to the pasha and my four captors had to appear before him. After the hearing, at which the testimony of the two witnesses was accepted, the verdict was that I must be set free, but the four robbers, who had violated the pashas' permits, were condemned to the Mediterranean galleys. Half of the money they had collected was to go to the state, but the other half was divided in two, one part for me, the other to ransom those who had been captured with me and sold into slavery. This judgment was not only publicly pronounced but carried out at once, so that I was now to be given my freedom, my coat and a goodly sum of money.

Once I had been released from the chains, in which my captors had dragged me round as a wild man, and was wearing my old coat again and had been given the money the pasha had allotted me, the resident or consul of every European nation wanted to take me home with him, the Dutch because they saw me as a fellow countryman but the others because I seemed to belong to their religion. I thanked them all because together, as good Christians, they had released me from my grotesque but also dangerous captivity. At the same time I was wondering what to do now I had, against my will, acquired a lot of money and many friends.

Chapter 19

My fellow countrymen persuaded me to dress differently and, since I had nothing to do, I made enquiries of all the Europeans who liked to see me and, out of Christian charity as well as to hear my strange stories, often used to invite me to their houses. Since there seemed little hope that the war in Syria and Judea would soon end and allow me to continue on my journey to Jerusalem, I changed my mind and decided to take passage to Portugal on a large merchantman that was ready to leave, with merchants on board who were travelling home; I would then make a pilgrimage to Santiago de Compostela instead of Jerusalem. After that I would settle down somewhere, living off what God granted me. And so that I could do this without going to great expense (for as soon as I had a lot of money, I started to scrimp and save) I came to an agreement with the leader of the Portuguese merchants that he should take all my money, use it for his own dealings and return it to me in Portugal; in the meantime, instead of paying interest he would let me eat at his table and take me home on his ship; in return I declared myself ready to perform any duties – on board or on land – that he might require of me. As it happened, I was counting my chickens before they were hatched because I had no idea what the good Lord had in store for me, and I was looking forward all the more to this long and dangerous journey because the previous one on the Mediterranean had gone so well.

Once we had sailed down the Red Sea we reached the ocean, where we had a favourable wind, and set course to round the Cape of Good Hope. The conditions were as good as we could have hoped for and we sailed on happily for several weeks. But when we thought we must be off Madagascar a hurricane arose so suddenly that we hardly had time to take in the sails. The longer it went on, the more violent the wind became, so that we had to cut down the mast and leave ourselves at the mercy of the waves, which now threw us up almost to the clouds and the next moment dropped us down into a trough. This lasted for a good half hour and certainly taught us to pray most fervently. Finally they threw us onto a submerged reef with such force that the ship broke into pieces with a terrible crash, setting off terrible cries and screams from the crew and passengers. In a trice the sea all round was covered in bales, chests and debris from the ship. Here and there you could see and hear unfortunate men, both on the surface and below, clinging on to anything they could get their hands on, wailing and commending their souls to God as they saw their end approaching.

A carpenter and I were lying on a fairly large portion of the ship that had retained some crossbeams we were holding on to and giving each other encouragement. The terrible wind gradually subsided so that the furious waves of the raging sea slowly calmed down. There followed a pitch-dark night with a terrible downpour so that it looked as if, out there in the

110

middle of the sea, we were to be drowned from above.

That lasted until midnight, during which time we were in dire straits, but then the sky cleared again so that we could see the stars. And from them we could tell that the longer the wind had been blowing, the farther away from the coast of Africa it had driven us towards the land of *Australia incognita*, at which we were very alarmed. Towards daybreak it became very dark again, so that we could hardly see each other, even though we were lying close together. In this darkness and our wretched state, we continued to drift until we suddenly realised that we had run aground and stopped. The carpenter had an axe in his belt; he used it to check the depth of the water and found that on one side it was less than a foot deep, which cheered us very much and gave us the sure hope that God had brought us to land somewhere. And this was confirmed by a pleasant odour we smelt once we had recovered somewhat. But since it was so dark, both of us exhausted and the daylight about to come very soon, we didn't have the heart to go down into the water and look for the land, even though we thought we could hear various birds singing, as actually turned out to be the case.

However, as soon as the longed-for daylight began to appear in the east, we saw through the gloom some land covered in bushes right in front of us, so we immediately went down into the water, which gradually grew shallower until, to our delight, we reached dry land. We fell to our knees, kissed the ground and thanked God for saving us and bringing us safely onto dry land. That is how I came to be on that island.

At that point we couldn't tell whether we were on an island or the mainland, whether it was inhabited or uninhabited, but what we did see was that the soil must be extremely fertile, for we were faced with bushes and trees, growing as thickly as hemp in a meadow, so that we could hardly make our way through. However, once it was fully light and we had gone through the bushes away from the shore for a quarter of an hour or so without seeing the slightest trace of human habitation, but here and there strange birds that didn't fly away from us but let us pick them up, we could plainly tell that we must be on an uninhabited but very fruitful island. We found lemons, oranges and coconuts, which were very refreshing, and when the sun rose we came to a plain which was covered in the kind of palm trees that can be used to make palm wine – which more than pleased my companion who was in the habit of drinking far too much of it.

We sat down in the sun there, took off our clothes and hung them on the trees to dry, then walked round in our vests. The carpenter struck a palm with his axe and was well rewarded with juice; but we had no vessels to catch it in and we had both lost our hats during the shipwreck.

Once our clothes were dry again we got dressed and climbed the rocky peak to the north, between the plain and the sea. From there we looked all round and established that we were indeed not on the mainland but on an island, which you could walk round in no more than an hour and a half. We were dismayed that we could not see any land, either near or far away, just the sea and the sky, and lost all hope of ever seeing people again. But on the other hand we were comforted by the fact that the good Lord had sent us to this safe and extremely fruitful place, not to one that was barren or inhabited by cannibals.

Then we started to think about what we should do, and since

we would have to live together as prisoners on this island, we vowed an oath to be faithful to each other. The aforementioned hill was not only full of all kinds of different birds but we were also amazed at the number of nests lying there. We drank some of the eggs and took more back with us, then on the way we found a spring of sweet water that flowed down the hill to the east with such force that it could have driven a small mill wheel before going into the sea. We were so delighted by this that we agreed to set up our home beside the spring.

To equip our new home we had nothing but an axe, one spoon, three knives, a fork and some scissors. My comrade did have a ducat or two, perhaps even thirty, which we would have willingly spent on a firesteel if there had been anywhere to buy one, but they were of no use to us. They were worth even less than my powder horn, that was still full of priming powder. It was like paste, so I dried it out in the sun, scattered some on a stone, put some easily combustible things on top of it – there was plenty of that, for example, moss and fibre from the coconut trees – struck the stone through it with the knife and thus made a fire, at which we were as delighted as we had been when we were saved from the sea. If we'd just had some salt, bread and vessels to hold our drink, we'd have thought ourselves the most fortunate men on earth, although twenty-four hours earlier we may have been among the most unfortunate. God is merciful, glory be to Him for ever and ever, amen.

We caught some of the fowls, of which there were so many walking round us unafraid, plucked them, washed them and put them on a wooden spit. I sat there turning the roast, while my comrade brought wood and made a hut where we could shelter if it should rain, because off the coast of Africa the rain from India is often very unhealthy. For the salt we lacked we substituted lemon juice to give some flavour to our food.

Chapter 20

That was the first meal we had on our island and, once we had finished it, we set about gathering dry wood to keep our fire going. We would have liked to explore our island straightaway but we were weary from our exertions and felt sleepy so we had to lie down and didn't wake up until the next morning. Once we saw that it was light, we followed our stream down to where it flowed into the sea. There we were astonished to see an incredible number of fish, the size of an average salmon or large carp, that were swimming up into the stream, attracted by the fresh water, looking as if a great herd of swine had been driven up there. And since we also came across some bananas and sweet potatoes that were excellent, we agreed it would be like the land of Cockaigne (although there were no four-footed animals there) if we only had some company to help us consume the fish and fowls of this splendid island. But we couldn't find a single sign of men ever having been there.

So we discussed how we should organise our domestic affairs, where we might find vessels in which we could cook our food or collect the palm juice and allow it to ferment, so that we could really enjoy it. We were walking along the shore talking about these matters when we saw something drifting along far out at sea but so far away that we could not make out what it was. In fact it looked bigger than it actually was, for when it came closer and was washed up on the shore, it turned out to be a half-dead woman lying on a chest, her hands gripping the handles. For the love of Christ, we pulled her onto dry land and, after we had come to the conclusion from her clothing and some signs on her face that she was an Abyssinian Christian, we tried even harder to help her regain consciousness. We stood her on her head, but treating her with propriety, as is right for respectable women in such circumstances, until a great deal of water had run off her; then, since we had nothing with us to bring her round, we kept pressing the enlivening moisture contained in the ends of the lemon rind under her nose and shaking her until she finally started to move and to speak Portuguese.

As soon as my comrade heard this and saw the colour come back to her cheeks, he said to me, "This Abyssinian woman was on our ship. She was the maid of a noble Portuguese lady, for I knew them well; they boarded in Macao and wanted to sail with us to the island of Annabon."

As soon as the woman heard him, she cheered up. She called him by his name and not only told us about her journey, but said how happy she was that both of them were still alive and should meet again on dry land and out of all danger. Then the carpenter asked her what goods there were in the chest, to which she replied that there were some pieces of Chinese cloth, a few guns and daggers and then various larger and smaller pieces of china that her master was to have sent to a prince in Portugal. We were delighted to hear this, because they were things we were most in need of. Then she asked us to be so good as to keep her with us, saying she would be happy to work as our maid, obey us as a slave and do the cooking, washing and other tasks, if we would only keep her under our protection and allow her to enjoy such life as nature provided here together with us.

After that the two of us, with a great deal of toil, dragged the chest to the place where we had chosen to live. There we opened it and found things that suited our needs perfectly, given our situation. We unpacked everything and dried the goods in the sun, in which our new cook proved a great help. After that we started to butcher the fowls, boil and roast them, and while the carpenter went to collect palm juice, I climbed up the mountain to gather eggs and boil them until they were hard so that we could use them instead of bread.

On my way I gave thanks to God for the great gifts His fatherly providence had granted us and provided for us to enjoy; I prostrated myself and, with arms outstretched and a full heart, said, "O, most gracious heavenly Father, now do I see that you are more willing to give than we to ask. Yes, O, beloved Lord, with the abundance of your divine riches you have granted us much more than we poor creatures were minded to ask of you. O, loving Father, may it please your infinite mercy to ensure that we use these your gifts and graces in no other way than is agreeable to your most holy will and satisfaction, and does honour to your great ineffable name, so that we, together with all the elect, may praise, laud and honour you here on earth and then in eternity."

With these and many more such words of devotion, all of which came from the very depths of my soul, I walked round until I had gathered all the eggs we needed and then returned to our hut, where our evening meal stood ready for us on the chest, that I and my comrade had fished out of the sea that day together with our cook, and now used in place of a table.

While I had been out looking for eggs my comrade, who was a young fellow of a little more than twenty while I was over forty, had come to an agreement with our cook that was to prove disastrous for both of us. Once I had left them alone together they had started to talk about the past, but also about the fruitfulness and use of this happy, more than blest island, and they became so intimate that they started to talk about a marriage between them. However the supposed Abyssinian woman said she would not consider it unless my comrade, the carpenter, made himself sole master of the island and got rid of me. It would, she said, be impossible to enjoy marriage together in peace if there were an unmarried man living together with them.

"Just you think," she went on to my comrade, "about how you would be tormented by suspicion and jealousy if you should marry me and the old man talked to me every day, even if it should never occur to him to cuckold you. However, I have a better idea: if I should ever marry and increase the number of people on this island (that can easily support more than a thousand) it would be preferable if it were the old man. For if that happened, it would only be twelve or at most fourteen years before we would have raised a daughter we could marry off to you. Even then you wouldn't be of the age the old man is now, and in the meantime the certain prospect of the one of you becoming the other's father-in-law and the other his son-in-law, would clear away any nasty suspicion, and any danger that might otherwise threaten me. Of course, it is natural that a young woman such as myself would rather take a young man than an old one, but we both have to reconcile ourselves to what our present circumstances demand to ensure my safety and that of those who might be born of me."

My good carpenter was so taken in and infatuated by all this (which went on much longer and in greater detail than I have here set out), by the beauty of the supposed Abyssinian woman, which by the fire in my comrade's eyes shone much more brightly than before, and her lively gestures, that he went so far as to say that he would rather throw the old man (meaning me) into the sea and destroy the whole island, than hand over a woman such as she. Thus the above-mentioned agreement was made between the two of them, to the effect that he would strike me down with his axe from behind or while I was asleep, because he was afraid of both my strength and my staff, that he had himself made as stout as any soldier's pikestaff.

After this compact had been made, she showed my comrade where, close to our hut, there was some fine potter's clay, out of which she was sure she could make some earthenware crockery in the manner of the Indian women who live on the coast of Guinea; she then talked of all kinds of plans as to how she would bring forth and sustain her family on this island, creating a life of peaceful sufficiency, even down to the hundredth generation. Then she went on and on praising her ability to make use of the coconut trees and the cotton they produce to make clothes for herself and all her children and children's children.

I, poor soul, arrived knowing nothing of this – for me disagreeable – agreement, and sat down to enjoy what had been prepared, even saying grace according to hallowed Christian usage. However, as soon as I made the sign of the cross over the food and my companions at table, both our cook and the chest vanished, including everything that had been in it, leaving behind such an awful stench that my comrade fainted.

Chapter 21

As soon as he had recovered and come back to his senses, he knelt down before me, put his hands together and for a good ten minutes said nothing but, "O my father! O my brother! O my father! O my brother!" And as he repeated these words, he started to cry in such heartfelt fashion that he couldn't say anything comprehensible for sobbing and I began to fear that the fright and stench must have sent him out of his mind. As he kept going on and asking me for forgiveness, I replied, "My dear friend, what should I forgive you since you've never insulted me at all? Just tell me how I can help you."

"I beg your forgiveness," he said, "because I have sinned against God, against you and against myself." And with that he started up his previous complaint and went on until I said I knew nothing bad about him, and if he had still done something that troubled his conscience, I would not only forgive him from the bottom of my heart but also, if he had transgressed against the Lord, join him in begging His compassion and forgiveness.

At this he grasped my legs, kissed my knees and gave me a look of such longing and sadness that I immediately fell silent and had no idea what could be the matter with the fellow. Then I took him in my arms, pressed him to my breast and asked him to tell me what was wrong and how I could help him. At this he confessed in detail to everything he had said to the supposed Abyssinian woman and what he had decided to do to me, both of which were against God, against nature and against the vow of faithful friendship we had solemnly sworn to each other. And he did this with words and gestures that made it easy to see and accept his fervent remorse and contrite heart.

I comforted him as well as I could and said that perhaps God had sent us this trial as a warning to be better prepared for the wiles and temptations of the Devil and to live out our lives in the fear of God. Because of his agreement to do evil, he certainly had cause to beg God's forgiveness from the bottom of his heart but, I went on, he had an even greater obligation to thank Him for His loving kindness and mercy in pulling him, like a loving father, out of the evil Devil's wiles and snares, saving him from damnation both in this world and the next. It would be necessary for us to be more cautious in the future than when we were living out in the world among people, for if either or both of us should fall, there would be no one here to help us back on our feet, apart from the dear Lord, whom we should bear in mind all the more, constantly begging Him for help and support.

He was somewhat comforted by such encouragement but still not entirely happy and humbly begged me to impose a penance on him for his sin. So in order to revive his depressed spirits, I said that since he was a carpenter and still had his axe with him, he should erect a cross at the place on the shore where our satanic cook had been washed up. That would not only be a penance pleasing unto God, but would ensure that the Evil One, who shrank from the sign of the cross, would not so easily invade our island again.

"O," he replied, "I won't make and erect just one cross on the low ground but two up on the mountain as well, if only, O my father, I can win your favour again and be assured of God's forgiveness."

Thus full of zeal, he went off straightaway and didn't stop until he had made three crosses, of which we erected one on the beach and the other two on top of the mountain, each in a separate spot and with the following inscription:

"In the name of Christ, this symbol of the sufferings of our Redeemer was made and erected here by Simon Meron, from Lisbon in Portugal, with the advice and help of his faithful friend Simplicius Simplicissimus, a German, to the glory of Almighty God and to spite the Enemy of the human race."

From that point on we started to live in a manner more pleasing to God than we had done previously and, so that we could keep the Sabbath and make it holy, I made a kind of calendar by cutting a notch in a stick every day and a cross on Sundays. Then we would sit together and talk of holy and divine matters. We had to do this because I had not yet been able to think of anything I could use instead of paper and ink to write down an account of our life.

To close this chapter I must recall a strange matter that very much alarmed and frightened us on the evening after our fine cook departed from us, but which we hadn't noticed on the first night because in our great weariness and tiredness we had been overcome with sleep. It was this: while we were still thinking about the thousand subterfuges, with which the accursed Devil tried to ruin us in the form of the Abyssinian woman, and therefore could not sleep but spent long hours awake, mostly in prayer, we saw, as soon as it grew dark, a countless crowd of lights floating round in the air and giving off such a bright glow that we could tell the fruits in the trees from the leaves. We thought it was a new trick of the Arch Enemy come to torment us again, so we lay there, still and quiet, until we eventually realised that they were a kind of firefly, or glow-worm as some people call them, that come from a strange type of rotten wood that grows on that island. They shine so brightly that you can even use them instead of a lighted candle, indeed, afterwards I often wrote parts of this book by their light. If they'd been as common in Europe, Asia and Africa as they were there, the candlemakers would be short of business.

Chapter 22

Now that we saw that we would have to stay where we were, we started to reorganise our household. Out of black wood, that was almost as hard as iron when it had dried out, my comrade made a spade and a hoe for each of us. The first thing we did with these was to set up the three crosses, then we diverted the sea into pools so that, as I had seen in Alexandria, it would turn into salt. Thirdly we started to make a pleasure garden, for we remembered that the Devil finds work for idle hands. Following that, we dug an extra course for the stream so that we could divert it whenever we wanted and, drying out the old stream, could gather as many fish and crabs as we liked without getting our hands or feet wet.

Then we discovered, close to the stream, some fine potter's clay. Although we didn't have a wheel, a drill or any other instruments we could use to make something like that, in order to turn the clay and make all kinds of crockery, we thought up something that allowed us to make the things we wanted. We kneaded the clay until it had the right consistency, then we rolled it out into strips about as thick and long as English tobacco pipes. These we coiled round on top of each other and shaped them into the kind of dishes we required, both large and small, pots and little cups for cooking and drinking, and once we had fired them successfully there was no longer anything we needed for although we lacked bread, we had plenty of dried fish that we used instead of bread.

With time our scheme for making salt also started to work so that we lacked for nothing but were living like folk in the earliest golden age. We also gradually learnt how to make tasty cakes instead of bread out of eggs, dried fish and lemon peel, which we rubbed between two stones to make fine flour then baked in the fat from the flightless dodos. And my comrade knew how to make the palm wine, leaving it standing in large pots for a few days until it fermented. He would then drink so much that he would stagger and reel, as he eventually did every day, though God knows how often I told him not to. He said that if it was left standing too long, it would turn into vinegar. There is some truth in that, so I said that in that case he shouldn't collect so much, just enough for our needs, to which he replied that it was a sin to scorn the gifts of God and, anyway, we had to bleed the palm trees from time to time so that they wouldn't suffocate in their own blood. Thus I had to let him give free rein to his craving, unless I wanted to hear him going on about me begrudging him things we had aplenty for free.

So we lived, as I said, like the first people in the golden age, when a benign Heaven made all kinds of good things grow out of the earth for them without their having to do any work themselves. But just as there is no life in this world that is so sweet and happy that it is not at times embittered by the gall of suffering, so it happened with us. Thus although our kitchen and cellar improved daily, our clothes became worse day by day until eventually they were rotting away on our bodies. The good thing for us was that so far we had not had a winter, in fact not even the least cool spell although by then, when we had to go naked, we had already spent a year and half on the island, according to the notches in my stick. All the time the weather was like that in Europe in May or June, except that around August there would be heavy rain and thunderstorms there; also here the days and nights do not get shorter or longer by more than a good hour and a quarter from one solstice to the next.

So although we were alone on this island, we didn't want to go naked, like brute beasts, but dressed like honest Christians from Europe. Had we had four-footed creatures here, then we could have used their hides but in their absence we skinned the larger birds, for example the dodos and penguins, and made breeches from them. Since, however, we lacked the necessary equipment and materials, we couldn't make them to last; they became hard, uncomfortable and fell apart in no time at all. We could get a kind of cotton from the coconut trees, but could neither spin nor weave it. However my comrade, who had spent several years in India, showed me something like a sharp thorn at the end of their leaves; if you break it off, and pull it along the rib of the leaf, in the way you string beans, then remove the side veins, you are left with the thorn and a thread attached, which you can use as a needle and thread. This gave me the possibility of making trousers for us from the same coconut leaves by sewing them together with the thread from their own plants.

While we now lived together and had reached the point where we had no cause to complain about overwork, shortages or despondency, my comrade continued to drink as he had begun and it was now his habit until finally his lungs and liver became inflamed and before I realised what was happening, he abandoned me, the island and the palm wine through an early death. I buried him as well as I could and, reflecting on the inconstancy of human life and other things, wrote the following epitaph:

> I lie buried here and not in the sea,
> Nor in Hell, because there were three
> Fighting for my soul: the first, the raging ocean,
> Then the prince of darkness, Satan,
> I escaped, for God His help did lend,
> But the third, palm wine, brought me to my end.

So I was left on my own, lord of the whole island, and resumed my hermit's life, not simply because of my situation but because I had the determination and will to do so. I did make use of the products the place provided, with heartfelt thanks to God, who in His goodness and omnipotence had granted me such a rich supply, while at the same time making sure that I did not misuse its abundance. I often wished I had with me honest Christians, who were suffering poverty and want elsewhere, to make use of the gifts of God here. Since, however, I knew that, if it were His divine will, God Almighty could easily have transported more people than me to this place, this frequently gave me cause to humbly thank Him for His divine providence that He had afforded me such fatherly sustenance before many thousands of others, and put me in such a calm and peaceful situation.

Chapter 23

My comrade had not been dead a week when I noticed that there had been a ghost round my hut.

"Well then," I thought, "you are all on your own, Simplicius, so why should the Evil One not presume to torment you? Don't you think that the malicious spirit will try to make your life a misery? But why do you bother with him when God is your friend? What you need is something to occupy yourself, otherwise idleness and the abundance here will bring about your downfall, for apart from him you have no enemy but yourself, and the abundance and pleasure of this island will only make you stronger in your fight with the one who thinks himself strongest of all. And should he be overcome with the help of God, then if God so wishes you will remain your own master through His grace."

I went around with these thoughts going through my head for a few days and they improved my state of mind somewhat and made me reverent, because I expected to have to endure an encounter I would doubtless have with the Foul Fiend. But in this I was deceiving myself, for when one evening I heard something making a noise, I went out of my hut, which was beside a rock in the mountain below which the freshwater stream ran down into the sea. There I saw my comrade standing by the wall of rock, scrabbling with his fingers in a crack. I was frightened, as you can well imagine, but I immediately plucked up my courage, made the sign of the cross to put myself under the protection of God and thought, "It has to be, so it is better to get over with it now."

At that I went across to the ghost and spoke the words that are usual in such circumstances, at which I immediately realised that it was my dead comrade who, while he was alive, had hidden his ducats there so that if a ship should ever come to the island he could recover them and take them with him. He then made it clear to me that he had put more trust in this small sum of money, which he had hoped would help to take him home, than in God, and had to atone for it with his unrest after his death and, against his will, cause me inconvenience. At his request I took out the money, though I thought it worth less that nothing, which you can well believe as there was nothing I could use it for.

That was the first fright I had now that I was alone, but afterwards I was attacked by quite different spirits than that one. I have nothing else to say about those except that, with God's help and grace, I came to the point where I had no enemy any more except for my own thoughts, which could be quite variable, for thoughts are not free, as people tend to say, since in due course we will have to account for them.

So that these should not stain my soul with sin, I not only made an effort to reject everything that was of no use, every day I assigned myself a physical task, which I had to carry out as well as my usual prayers. For man is born to work, as a bird is to fly, and idleness brings sickness to both the soul and the body and, when you're least aware of it, ultimate perdition. Therefore I planted a garden, of which I had no need at all, given that the whole island was a delightful pleasure garden; in fact all I did was to put this or that in better order, though many people might find the natural disorder of the plants as they grew together more charming; then, as I said above, I abolished idleness, for does not the Devil find work for idle hands?

O how often did I wish, when my limbs were weary and needed rest, that I had some godly books to comfort, delight and instruct me, but I had none at all. However, before I came here I had read about a saintly man, who said that the whole world was a big book, in which he could see the marvels God had created and thus be encouraged to praise Him anew. I therefore determined to follow him, even though I was no longer in the world, as you might say; this little island had to be the whole world for me in which everything, even a tree, had to be an encouragement to piety and a reminder of the kind of thoughts a true Christian ought to have.

So: if I saw a prickly plant, I remembered Christ's crown of thorns; if I saw an apple or a pomegranate, I thought about the fall of our first parents and bemoaned it; if I extracted palm juice from a tree I saw in my mind's eye my merciful Redeemer shedding his blood down the shaft of the cross for me; if I saw the sea or a mountain I recalled the miracles our Saviour had performed in such places; if I found one or two stones that were right for throwing, I imagined the Jews wanting to stone Christ; and when I was in my garden I thought about his agonised prayer on the Mount of Olives, or about Christ's sepulchre, or how he appeared to Mary Magdalen after the resurrection. I went over these and similar thoughts daily, I never ate without thinking of Christ's Last Supper and never cooked anything without the fire reminding me of the eternal torments of Hell.

I eventually found that it was possible to write on a kind of large palm leaf with the sap of fernambuco wood, of which there are several species on this island, mixed with lemon juice. I was very pleased at this, for now I could compose and write down proper prayers. And then finally, when I looked back over my life and the villainies I had committed from my earliest days and considered how the merciful Lord, despite all those gross sins, had so far not only preserved me from eternal damnation but given me time to mend my ways, in order to beg His forgiveness and thank Him for his goodness towards me, I wrote everything that occurred to me in this book I made from the palm leaves and put it in this place, together with the ducats my comrade left behind, so that if people should eventually come here, they would find it and learn who had lived on this island before them.

If, today or tomorrow, before or after my death, someone should find and read this, I would ask them, if they find words in it that are not becoming in speech, never mind in writing, not to be angry at that, but to bear in mind that relating lively stories and events demands appropriate words to put them across; and just as the maidenhair fern does not easily become wet from the rain, nor does an honest, pious mind become infected, poisoned and corrupted from any narrative, however frivolous it may sound. An open-minded Christian reader will rather be amazed and praise God's mercy when they discover that such a bad lot as myself still found the grace in His eyes to withdraw from the world and live in such a way that he can hope to come to eternal glory and to achieve the bliss of eternal life after the sacred sufferings of the Redeemer through a blessed END.

A report on Simplicissimus by Joan Cornelissen, a Dutch ship's captain from Harlem, to his good friend German Schleiffheim von Sulsfort.

Chapter 24

You will doubtless remember very well how I promised when I departed to bring back to you the greatest rarity I found in India or during our voyage. Now I have collected some unusual plants from the sea and the land with which you can decorate your cabinet of curiosities but what seems to me most astonishing and worth preserving is this book, in which a German living alone on an island out in the ocean made, for lack of paper, out of palm leaves, and wrote a description of his whole life in it. I will have to go into some detail of how I came by this book and what kind of man the aforesaid German was, even though he does go on at some length about it in his book.

Once we had completed loading in the Moluccas and set sail for the Cape of Good Hope we noticed that our journey home was not going to be as fast as we had initially hoped, for the wind was mostly against us and so variable that for a long time we were driven round and held up. This meant that all the ships in the convoy had many men who were sick, so our admiral fired a shot and raised a flag to tell all the captains in the fleet to come to his ship. We discussed the situation and decided to head for the island of St Helena, where the sick could be refreshed, and wait there for some decent weather. If it should happen that our convoy was dispersed by storm, the first ships to reach that island were to wait two weeks there for the others. All this was thought through and agreed on.

What we had feared did then happen. The fleet was so scattered by a storm that no two ships were in sight of each other. With my ship alone and an adverse wind, a lack of fresh water and many sick men, I had to tack, but that was not much use; I estimated that St Helena was four hundred miles away and we would have needed the wind to change in order to reach it.

Sailing thus to and fro, with the sick men getting worse and their numbers increasing, we saw far away to the east what we thought was a single rock and made our course towards it, hoping to find some land in the area, even though there was none marked there on our charts. As we approached this rock from the north, it looked to us as if it was a high, stony, infertile mountain standing there by itself in the ocean and that it would be impossible to climb or even disembark on that side. But we could tell from the smell that we must be close to some good land. The mountain had many birds perching on and flying round it, and while we were observing them we saw two crosses on the highest peak. It was obvious that they had been put there by human hand, which meant it must be possible to climb the mountain, so we sailed round it and found on the other side a small but very pleasant tract of countryside such as I had never seen in the East or the West Indies. We made anchor at ten fathoms and sent a boat with eight men to see if there were any fresh supplies to be had there.

They soon returned, bringing with them an abundance of fruits of all kind, for example lemons, pomegranates, coconuts, bananas, sweet potatoes and, what pleased us most, the news that there was excellent drinking water on the island; and although they had met a German, who appeared to have been there for a long time, the place was still so full of fowls that could be caught by hand that they had filled the boat with them and killed them with sticks. They thought the German must have been guilty of some misdeed on a ship and set down on the island in punishment, which we assumed as well. They also said the man was not in his right mind but must be a complete idiot, for they had not been able to have any conversation with him at all.

This news cheered up all the men on the ship, especially the sick, and everyone wanted to go on land to refresh themselves. So I sent one boat after the other there, not just the sick to recover their health, but also to get fresh water for the ship, both of which were urgent, so that most of us went onto the island, where we found what was more like an earthly paradise than a desolate unknown place!

I also realised at once that the German could not be the fool, even less the miscreant, our men had initially thought. He had marked all the trees that had smooth bark with Biblical and other fine sayings, to cheer up his Christian spirit and raise his mind up to God. And where there were no sayings there were at least the four letters above Christ on the cross, that is INRI, or the name JESU and Maria, or simply an instrument of the sufferings of Christ, from which we surmised that he must definitely be a Papist, because it all looked very papistical to us. In one place there was the Latin *memento mori*, in another the Hebrew *Ieschua Hanosri Melech Haijehudim*, and elsewhere the same kind of thing in Greek, German, Arabic or Malay (which language is spoken throughout India) the sole purpose of which was to remind himself of the divine heavenly things in Christian fashion.

We also found his comrade's grave and epitaph, that the German describes in the story of his life, and also the third cross that the two of them erected on the sea shore, which led to the ship's company calling the place the Cross Island, mainly because we found the sign of the cross cut into all the trees. But for all of us his short, ingenious maxims were like dark, puzzling oracles from which we could tell that their author was no fool but must be a clever poet and, especially, a pious Christian who spent much of his time reflecting on heavenly matters. The ship's chaplain, who accompanied me and wrote down a lot of the things he found, thought that the following rhyme was the best, perhaps because it was something new to him. It went:

Oh, our sovereign blessing! Thou liv'st in such dark light
That the very clarity obscures Thy glory bright.

At this the chaplain, who was a very learned man, said, "A man in this world could get that far, but no higher, unless God of His grace wanted to reveal more of the greatest good to him."

137

Meanwhile the men from the ship who were in good health were going over the whole island to gather refreshments for themselves and the sick, and to look for this German, whom all the officers had a great desire to see and talk with. But they couldn't find him, though they did find a huge cave in the rock, full of water; they surmised he must be in there because there was a fairly narrow footpath leading into it, but the darkness and the water were such that they couldn't enter it themselves. They did light torches and pitch wreaths, so that they could examine the cave, but these went out before they had penetrated half a stone's throw, so all the trouble they went to was in vain.

Chapter 25

The men told me about their wasted efforts and I decided to go myself to look at the place and see if anything could be done to get hold of the German, but then a strong earthquake arose, that made the men think the whole island was about to sink at any moment, and if that wasn't enough, I was called urgently to the rest of the crew on the island who were in a very strange and worrying state: one was standing there, sword drawn fighting a tree, saying he had the biggest of giants to contend with; in another place one was staring up at the sky, with joy written all over his face, telling the others he could see God and the whole heavenly host; another was looking at the ground, in fear and trembling, claiming he was looking down into a terrible pit in front of him where he could see the Devil himself and all his minions swarming round; another had a club and was swinging it so that no one dared approach him, at the same time shouting that they should come and help him against all the wolves that wanted to tear him apart; then there was one sitting on a water butt, that we had brought to repair and fill with water, and spurring it on as if he wanted to ride it like a horse; farther away one was fishing with a rod on dry land and pointing out to another all the fish that were going to bite.

All in all it seemed that each one had his own idea in his head that had nothing to do with those of the others. One came running up to me and said, "In the name of a thousand gods, Captain, I beg you to see that justice is done and protect me from these terrible fellows!"

When I asked who had offended him, he pointed at the others, who were behaving as madly and crazily as he was, and replied, "These tyrants want to make me eat up two tons of herring, six Westphalian hams and twelve Dutch cheeses together with a ton of butter, all at once. But Captain," he went on, "how can that be? It's impossible and I'd choke or burst!"

They were all going around with these and other similar fancies and it would have been quite amusing if I'd only been sure it would all come to an end with no harm done. But I and the others who were still in our right minds were really worried, in particular because the longer it went on the more of these crazy men there were and we had no idea how long we ourselves would remain free of this bizarre condition.

Our chaplain, who was a gentle, quiet man, and some of the others maintained that the German, whom the crew had encountered at first on the island, must be a holy man, pleasing unto God, and since our men had ruined the place where he dwelt by chopping down trees, picking fruits and killing the fowls, this punishment had been visited on us from above. There were others, though, who said he could be a magician who, with his art, was tormenting us with earthquakes and this kind of madness to get us to leave all the sooner, or even to destroy us entirely. It would be best, they said, to take him captive and compel him to bring our men back to their right minds. In this disagreement each man expressed his own opinion, both of which frightened me, for I thought, "If he is God's friend and this punishment has been visited on us for his sake, then God will presumably also protect him from us. If, however, he is a magician and can make us see such things and feel them in our bodies, then he will doubtless be able to do more so that we will not be able to catch him. And who knows, perhaps he is among us now, invisible?"

Eventually we did decide to go and find him and take him, either by persuasion or force. Therefore we went back to the cave with torches and pitch wreaths and candles in our lanterns, but we suffered the same fate as the others before: we could not take any light inside and, however hard we tried, could not progress any farther because of the water, darkness and sharp rocks. At this some started to pray, others to swear and curse, and we didn't know what to do or not do, in order to deal with our fears.

While we were standing in the dark cave with no idea what to do – that is we were all doing nothing but bewail our situation – we heard the German shouting to us from far away in the dark cave. "Gentlemen," he said, "why are you making such vain efforts to see me or to come in for some other reason? Can you not see that it is absolutely impossible? If you are not content with the refreshments God is giving you in this land but want to become rich from me, a poor, naked man, who possesses nothing but his life, I can tell you that you are wasting your time. Therefore I beg you in the name of Christ our Redeemer, to abandon your plan. Refresh yourself with the fruits of the island and leave me here in my safe refuge, to which your threatening remarks, which I could not but hear in my hut last night, made me flee, before you bring disaster upon yourselves, which God forbid."

We had no idea what to say to this, but our good chaplain shouted back to him at the top of his voice, "If someone molested you yesterday, then we are heartily sorry for that; it was done by the coarse seamen, who know nothing of good behaviour. We have not come to plunder or to take booty, but to ask your advice about how to help our men, most of whom have gone out of their senses on this island. Apart from that we would also like to talk with you, as a Christian and fellow countryman, and, following the last commandment of our Redeemer, render unto you all love, honour, loyalty and friendship and, if you would like, take you back to your home country with us."

To this he replied that he had clearly heard how we were disposed towards him the previous day, but he was willing to follow the law of our Saviour and return good for evil and not withhold from us how to help our men to recover from their crazy delirium: we should get those who were in this state to eat the stones of the plums with which they had eaten away all their sense and they would all improve in no time at all. We should, he said, have been able to tell that from the plums, without his advice, because if you ate the hot kernels along with them it would counteract the harmful cold of the plums. Since we perhaps didn't know the trees that bore that kind of plum, we should just beware of those on which was written:

> Be thou amazed at the fruit I bore,
> I am like Circe, the bewitching whore.

From this reply and what the German had said before, we felt assured that he had been frightened by the first crew members we had sent to the island and thus felt compelled to withdraw to this cave. We also saw that he must be a true, honest German since, regardless of the fact that he had been molested by our men, he still told us what had made our men go out of their minds and how they could be brought back to their senses. We immediately regretted the evil thoughts and wrong assumptions we had had about him, as a result of which we had quite rightly been punished and ended up in this dangerous dark cave from which it seemed impossible to get out without light because we had ventured much too far in.

Our chaplain therefore raised his voice again, speaking in most pitiful tones, "O, honest fellow countryman! Those who insulted you yesterday with their coarse language are very rough, indeed the coarsest fellows from our ship. Here now, on the other hand, are the captain and the principal officers, who have come to beg your forgiveness, to bring you friendly greetings and to give you anything that it is in our power to provide that may be of some use to you. And indeed, if you wish, we will take you away from this dreary solitude and back to Europe with us."

However, the only answer we got was that he thanked us very much for our generous offer but was not of a mind to accept anything we could give him. So far he had for fifteen years enjoyed living in this place by the grace of God and without any human help or company, so he had no desire to return to Europe and exchange his present contented state for such a long and dangerous journey to a place of constant, restless misery.

Chapter 26

After we had heard this we would have been happy to leave
the German where he was, if we could only have got out of his
cave. But that was impossible, for we could not do it without
light and we could not expect any help from the men who
were still charging round the island in their madness. We were
therefore very much afraid and were trying our best to persuade
the German to help us get out of the cave. But he ignored all
our arguments until finally, even though we reminded him
most movingly of our situation and that of our men, none of
whom could help the others without his help, and protested
before Almighty God, that in his stubbornness he would make
us die and that he would have to answer for it before God on
Judgment Day. And anyway, we added, if he refused to help
us get out of the cave alive, he would eventually have to drag
us out once we were dead and decaying; and then he would
be concerned to find enough dead men on the island who had
good cause to cry for eternal revenge on him for not coming
to their aid before they had perhaps, as was to be feared,
torn each other apart in their madness. This consideration
finally managed to get him to agree to lead us out of the cave,
though first of all we had promise to stick firmly, truly and

unwaveringly, in Christian faith and the old, honest German way, to the following five points:

Firstly: that we should not punish, either in word or deed, those we sent at first onto the island for what they had done to him;

Secondly: that on the other hand the fact that he, the German, had hidden from us and refused to answer our pleas and requests for such a long time, should be forgotten, dead and buried;

Thirdly: that we would not constrain him, as a free man who was subject to no one, to return to Europe with us;

Fourthly: that we would not leave any of our men behind on the island;

Fifthly: that we will not inform anyone, either in writing or by word of mouth, much less with a map, where and on what degree of latitude or longitude the island lies.

After we had sworn to stick to those points, he immediately showed himself to us with many lights that shone out in the darkness like bright stars; we could clearly see that they were not on fire because his hair and beard were full of them and would have burnt if they had been. Therefore we assumed they were pure carbuncles, a gem that is said to shine in the dark. Then he came down the rocks, one after the other, and had to wade through water in some places, following such strange twists and turns, as he approached us, that we would have been unable to find the way, even if we had had lights such as he had. It all seemed more like a dream than a true story and the German more like a ghost than a real man, with the result that some among us thought we had been taken with some crazy delirium, like our men on the island.

He had to spend so much time climbing up and down that it took him half an hour to reach us, but once he had, he shook each of us by the hand, in the German fashion, bade us a friendly welcome and asked us to forgive him for his distrust, that had made him keep us waiting for so long before leading us out into the light of day. Then he gave each of us one of his lights, which were not precious stones, but black beetles, the same size as the stag beetles in Germany. On the underside of their necks they had a white spot, the size of a pfennig piece, that shone in the darkness brighter than any candle, and with these curious lights we were glad to make our way out of the terrible cave together with our German.

He was a tall, strong, well-built man with straight limbs, a fine, bright complexion, coral lips, lively black eyes, a high, clear voice, long black hair and a full beard, both speckled with very little grey. His hair hung down over his hips and his beard right down to his navel; he had an apron of palm leaves round his private parts and a broad hat woven out of rushes on his head, held by a rubber band and thus protecting him like an umbrella from both the rain and the sun. All in all, he looked more or less the way the Papists generally portray their Saint Onofrius.

He refused to talk to us in the cave, but once he was out he told us why: if one made a loud noise there, it shook the whole island and caused such an earthquake that anyone on it would think it was about to sink under the waves, and he had often tried it out when his comrade was still alive. It reminded us of the hole in the ground not far from Vyborg in Finland that Johann Rauh writes about in chapter 22 of his *Cosmographia*. He added that we had gone in recklessly, telling us that he and his comrade had spent a whole year before exploring the way in, which would have been completely impossible, however long they spent, without the beetles, since all fire goes out in there.

By now we were approaching his hut, that our men had plundered and destroyed, which grieved me very much. He, however, looked at it coolly, doing nothing to suggest that it had caused him distress; in fact he comforted me, saying it had happened against my will and command; whether fate or command, it came from God, perhaps to tell him how far he should take pleasure in the presence and company of men, especially of Christians, in particular his European fellow countrymen. The booty the destroyers had taken from his poor dwelling would not be more than thirty ducats, which he was glad to let them have. His greatest loss, on the other hand, was a book in which he had taken great pains to describe the whole course of his life and how he had come to be on the island; but he could easily get over that because he could make another, as long as we didn't chop down all the palm trees and spared his life. Then he remembered that we had to hurry in order to be in time to help those who had lost their reason by eating the plums.

So we went to the where the plum trees were, which was also where our men, both the sick and the healthy, had made their camp. It was a strange sight that greeted us – not a single one of them was in his right mind. Those who were still sane had gone, fleeing from the madmen either by going back on board the ship or to some other place on the island. The first we ran into was a master gunner who was crawling on all fours, grunting like a pig and repeating, "Malt, malt," all the time. Thinking he had turned into a pig, he was telling us we should give him some malt to eat. The German advised us to give him a few kernels from the plums that had made them all lose their wits, promising that he would regain them when he'd eaten them. Once he'd done that, and even before they had got really warm inside him, he stood up and started to talk rationally; and by this means we had cured all the others in less than an hour. You can well imagine how delighted I was and told the German how obliged I was to him, since without his advice and help all of us, together with the ship and cargo, would without a shadow of a doubt have been lost.

Chapter 27

Since things were now satisfactory again, I had the trumpeter sound the call for the crew to assemble, for the few who had retained their sanity were, as I said, scattered over the island. Once they were gathered together I found that, for all the strange happenings, we had not lost a single man. Therefore our chaplain gave a beautiful sermon in which he extolled God's miracles, but above all praised the German, who listened with an almost annoyed look on his face, so highly that the sailor who had taken his book and thirty ducats, brought them back of his own accord and laid them at his feet. However, he refused to accept the money but asked me to take it back to Holland and give it to the poor in memory of his dead comrade. "Even if I had loads of money," he said, "I wouldn't have any use for it." As far as the present book is concerned, which you are now reading, he gave it to me as a memento of our meeting.

I had some arrack, Spanish wine, a couple of Westphalian hams, rice and other things brought, then roasted or boiled, to make a banquet for the German and to honour him, but he took very little, and that from the worst dishes which, as people say, is entirely contrary to the Germans' nature and habits. Our men had drunk all his supply of palm wine, so he made do with water and refused both the Spanish and the Rhine wine, though he was happy to see how merry we were. His greatest pleasure was talking to the sick, all of whom he consoled with the prospect of a speedy recovery. He was happy, he said, at having been able to serve people for once, in particular Christians and, above all, his fellow countrymen, something that had been denied him for many a year. He was both their cook and doctor, having long discussions with our physician and barber about what needed to be done for this or that man, for which both the officers and men idolised him.

For myself I was wondering what I might do to be of service to him. I kept him occupied and, without him knowing, had our carpenters make a new hut for him like the summerhouses we have at home, for I saw that he merited something much better than I could give him or than he would accept. His conversation was very pleasing but much too brief and whenever I asked him something about himself, he would direct me to the present book, saying that on that subject he had written more than enough, thinking about which now grieved him. But when I told him he should nevertheless go back to live among people and not end his days dying like a brute beast, for which he had a good opportunity now, he replied, "My God, what do you have in mind? There is peace here, war there; here I see nothing of pride, greed, wrath, envy, jealousy, deceit, nothing of all the worries about food and clothing, nor about honour and repute; here is a quiet, lonely place, without anger, quarrels and strife; a place secure from vain desires, a stronghold against all dissolute lust, protection against the many snares of the world, and quiet calm in which you can serve the All-Highest alone, contemplate His marvels, laud and praise Him.

"When I was still living in Europe, everything (O, woe is me that I must say this of Christians!) was full of war, fire, murder, robbery, plundering, the raping of women and maidens. But when God in His goodness rid us of those afflictions, as well as the terrible pestilence and the cruel famine, and gave the poor oppressed people peace once more, all the vices such as lust, greed, drinking and gambling, whoring and adultery returned, bringing all the other vices with them, until eventually it came to the point where some people were openly trying to make themselves great by oppressing the others, and any trick, deceit or calculating artifice was good enough for them. And what is worst of all is that there is no hope of improvement; they all imagine that if they just go to church once a week when they feel like it, and make their peace with God once a year, or so they think, they have not only done everything expected of a devout Christian but that God is in their debt for all their lukewarm devotions. Should I desire to go back to such people? Should I not be concerned that if I left this island, to which God has so miraculously brought me, I would suffer the same fate as Jonah out at sea? No!" he said, "God forbid I should do that."

Now that I had seen that he had no desire at all to leave with us, I started a conversation about something else and asked him how, living all on his own, he managed to feed himself and organise his life all by himself. For example was he not afraid, living so many hundreds and thousands of miles away from other Christians; in particular did he not wonder who, when his hour of death was at hand, would comfort him, pray for him, not to mention provide the help he would need if he were ill? Would he not, alone in the world, have to die like a wild animal or cattle?

He replied that, as far as food was concerned, in his loving-kindness God provided him with more than a thousand people could consume; for each month of the year he had a different kind of fish to eat, that came to spawn in or by the island's fresh water; he also enjoyed God's blessing in the birds that came down near him from time to time, either to rest, to eat or to lay their eggs and hatch out their young, to say nothing of the fruitfulness of the island that I could see for myself. As for the lack of people to help him in the hour of his farewell to the world, that did not concern him in the least, if he had God as his friend. As long as he had been among men in the world, he had always had more annoyance from enemies than pleasure from friends, and even friends often caused one more trouble than you would expect from a friendship. If he had no friends here to love and serve him, at least he had no enemies who hated him; and both of those kinds of men could cause you to sin, but being spared both, he could serve God all the more calmly. It was true that at the beginning he had had to suffer and overcome temptations both from himself and from the Arch Enemy of all mankind but he had ever found and received help, comfort and salvation through God's grace in the wounds of his Redeemer, which was still his sole refuge.

I spent my time with the German in several such and similar conversations. Meanwhile our sick men were getting better by the hour, so that after four days none was still ailing. We mended everything on the ship that needed mending, took on water and other things from the island and, after having enjoyed six days there and refreshed ourselves, set sail on the seventh for the island of St Helena, where we found some ships from our fleet that were also tending their sick while waiting for the other ships. From there we then made our way safely home to Holland.

With this letter you will also receive a few of the shining insects, which I often used to accompany the German to the cave, which is a terrifying cave of curiosities; it was well provided with eggs which, as the German told me, kept there for a year because the place is cool rather than cold. In the farthest corner of the cave he had hundreds of these beetles, which made it as light as a room with a superfluity of candles. He told me that at a certain time of the year they grow out of a particular kind of wood but are all eaten within a few weeks by species of birds that come to the island at the same time and hatch out their young. Then he has to find a way of keeping them in the cave to use instead of candles. There they retain their power for a whole year; out in the open air, however, the shining dampness quickly dries out so that they give off no light once they have been dead for a week.

The German had explored the cave with the help of these beetles alone and made it into such a safe refuge that even if we had a hundred thousand men there was no human force that could have brought him out against his will. When we left we gave him a burning-glass, so that he could light a fire using the sun's rays. It was the only thing he begged us to give him but, although he didn't want to accept anything from us, we left an axe, a spade, a hoe, two lengths of cotton from Bengal, half a dozen knives, a pair of scissors, two copper pots – and a pair of rabbits, to see if they would multiply on the island – after which we bade each other a very friendly farewell. I believe this island must be the healthiest place in the world, for all our sick men recovered within five days and the German had not been troubled by any illness the whole time he had been there.

The End

Conclusion

Dear esteemed etc reader,

I hereby testify that this *Simplicissimus* is a book by Samuel Greifsnon von Hirschfeld, for I not only found it among his papers after his death, but he himself also refers in this book to *Chaste Joseph*, that he wrote, and in his *Satirical Pilgrim* to this *Simplicissimus*, that he partly wrote while he was a musketeer in his young days. What I do not know is why he changed his name by rearranging the letters and put 'German Schleiffheim von Sulsfort' on the title page instead. He has also left more excellent satirical poems which, if this work should become popular, can also then be brought out in print. I wanted the reader to be aware of this and didn't want to hold back this conclusion because he published the first five parts during his life. Farewell reader.

Rheinnec, 22nd April 1668

H. I. C. V. G.
Magistrate of Cernheim

Simplicissimus – Johann Grimmelshausen

'This is Germany's first-ever bestseller, republished and translated more than 200 times. Brecht took Mother Courage out of it, and it receives a mention in one of John Le Carre's novels. It is a violent and often all-too-realistic picaresque, set in war-torn Europe during the 17th-century Thirty Years War. Simplicissimus is the eternal innocent, the simple-minded survivor, and we follow him from a childhood in which he loses his parents to the casual atrocities of occupying troops, through his own soldiering adventures, and up to his final vocation as a hermit alone on an island. It is Rabelasian in some respects, but more down to earth and melancholy.'

Phil Baker in *The Sunday Times*

'It is the rarest kind of monument to life and literature, for it has survived almost three centuries and will survive many more. It is a story of the most basic kind of grandeur – gaudy, wild, raw, amusing, rollicking and ragged, boiling with life, on intimate terms with death and evil – but in the end, contrite and fully tired of a world wasting itself in blood, pillage and lust, but immortal in the miserable splendour of its sins.'

Thomas Mann

'Grimmelshausen's *Simplicissimus* is one of the great picaresque novels. Like Cervantes and Halek, Grimmelshausen invented a naïve, feckless hero with a guiless yet lovable persona whose innocent wisdom shows up fully the world around him, Simplicissimus comes to symbolise sanity in a depraved, degenerate Europe torn apart by the Thirty Years War, and the novel, besides being funny, was German Baroque literature's most powerful plea for peace... *Simplicissimus* has been well served in English. At least eight translations have appeared to date. Mike Mitchell's new one is the raciest and most readable of all, the one most likely to appeal to a contemporary reader.'

Jeremy Adler in The London Review of Books

'Mitchell's brilliant translation of *Simplicissimus* updated the earlier, stilted English-language version by S Goodrich from 1912. Mitchell caught the vigour of the voice which, although conversational in tone, also has some subtle stylistic shifts. Mitchell shares Grimmelshausen's lightness of touch and conveys the energy of a narrator thinking on his feet.'

Eileen Battersby in The Irish Times

£10.99 ISBN 978 1 903517 42 0 434p B. Format

The Life of Courage – Johann Grimmelshausen

'A rich, sly entertainment.'   *Kirkus Reviews*

'This is one of the jauntiest literary romps ever written; admirers of Fielding will love it. Be warned, she is a likeable, amoral and versatile rogue – predating Daniel Defoe's *Moll Flanders* (1722) by 52 years. Her voice is candid, convincing, outrageously funny and more consistently sustained than Moll's. Courage is no victim of circumstances, she never courts sympathy. Regardless of what she does, the reader cheers her on.'   Eileen Battersby in *The Irish Times*

'Set during the Thirty Years War, which ripped apart 17th-century Europe, it is a glorious romp telling the story of Courage, a Bohemian girl whose town is overrun. Refusing to become part of the booty, she first survives, then thrives, following the armies and marrying a succession of officers, who are all killed. She uses charm and beauty to live life on her terms… The novel is a piece of history itself. Not only does it follow the war through its chronology, it makes a wonderful case for an independent woman who enjoys an awful lot of sex with whoever takes her fancy, particularly handsome army officers. While this novel, like the later *Moll Flanders*, was written by a man, its portrayal is of a remarkably modern woman shackled by the times. Courage did not solely use her beauty, she runs a canteen and traded. Above all she understood through her multiple marriages that she had to keep her own money.'
                    Scarlet MccGuire in *Tribune*

'Nobody would read this book for moral edification, but as an entertaining narrative, spiced with pornography and obscenity, in which a feisty woman uses all her resources to survive in a brutal world. Mike Mitchell, who has also translated Grimmelhausen's masterpiece *Simplicissimus*, provides a lively rendering of this difficult text.'

Ritchie Robertson in *The Times Literary Supplement*

£8.99 ISBN 978 1 910213 24 7 168 p B. Format

Tearaway – Johann Grimmelshausen

'Johann Grimmelshausen was born in early 17th-century Germany and fought in the Thirty Years War before becoming a writer, flavouring his memoirs with a sense of the fantastical story and fascinating yarn. *Tearaway* is the sequel to the German classic *Simplicissimus* which recounted the life of the author in the war and his many escapades across Europe involving his wife, fellow soldiers and any number of unlikely characters from the west coast of France to the eastern borders of Turkey. Eventually destined to live his remaining days as a one legged fiddler begging, stealing and cheating his way across his homeland he certainly lived a life getting there, however unlikely some of the tales he tells may be.'

Buzz Magazine

'*Tearaway* first published in 1670, is the third Johann Grimmelshausen novel to feature Simplicius and tells of the further encounters and exploits of this rather brazen traveller, with the horrors of the Thirty Years War looming in the background. Written in a direct narrative, the prose is just as engaging 333 years on.'   Ian Maxen in *What's on in London*

£6.99 ISBN 978 1 903517 18 5   168 p B. Format